# Curve Ball

BY JEROME G. SILBERT

CURVE BALL

Jerome G. Silbert

Copyright © 2017 Jerry Silbert

# Dedication

This book is dedicated to my parents, Jack and Liza and my in-laws, Irv and Jane. They were the victims of the worst in man, but held dear the dream of the best in humankind. Out of ashes, they not only survived but built a full and worthy life. Their memory is a blessing.

# *Chapter One*

# **2015 - Chicago**

"Where's the Yankee killer?"

"He's got a private cell. You know…away from the riff-raff. Lemme see." The lock-up keeper put his glasses on and ran his finger down a list of prisoners. "Cell 14. You wanna see him?"

Officer Sullivan hesitated. "Why not? Won't cost me anything."

Billy Dee Jackson, a large Black man in his sixties, took his set of keys from his desk. "You know, I've been down here a long time. Seen everything from punks and gang-bangers to politicians and people rolling in dough. Nothin' surprises me. No sir. I'll tell you one thing, I treat everyone the same. I talk softly so they have to listen. I don't come at them. They don't expect it. I tell 'em, it ain't my fault you're here. I've got no beef with you and you shouldn't have one with me. I'm goin' to keep you safe while you in my jail. But if I get lip, I give it back. You cool, I treat you good." He turned to Officer Sullivan. "Capeesh?"

He nodded. "Makes sense to me."

Billy Dee suffered from a slight limp. He had been on the force for forty years. Back then, Black cops were rare and his assignments reflected it. He had to give it to old Mayor Daley. At least he opened the door. Billy Dee smiled

1

at the places he had been. He'd directed traffic in the alley behind police headquarters at 11th and State. He'd frozen his balls off but didn't quit. After a year, he was transferred to the 2nd District night shift on the South Side before urban renewal. He had to climb those vertical death traps called the Robert Taylor Homes.

Now he hummed as he moved toward the metal door. "Whatcha want to see him for?" he asked Sullivan.

"It's not every day there's a celebrity in the hoosegow. Besides, a new season is coming. Maybe he could give me some pointers."

Billy Dee laughed. "You're in for a surprise." He stuck a big metal key into the lock and turned it. "He's down the corridor and to the left."

"Thanks." Sullivan started down the hallway not knowing what to expect.

*** 

The fluorescent lights in the hallway of the 19th District jail gave off a yellowish glow. Sullivan walked down the corridor and couldn't help noticing the smell that no amount of disinfectant could hide: a combination of stale air, human sweat, and unflushed waste. Eyes of despair and anger peeked out from the slots in the doors he passed.

"Hey, officer, I wants to call my lawyer," someone said.

"Yo officer, the son-of –a bitch really wants to call his momma or his bitch," another prisoner called out and started to laugh. "While you at it, I could use a bitch too. Man, what I'd do with a bad-ass bitch."

"Shut the fuck up, you wouldn't do nothin', shithead," another inmate said.

Sullivan ignored the noise. He got to Cell 14. The door slid open. Rakow sat on the floor next to the toilet. His knees were pulled up and his torso was bent forward. He didn't move.

"Jack Rakow?" Sullivan asked. His voice was edged with surprise. The figure on the floor of the cell was not the lengthy-legged young man whose image was plastered on long-ago baseball cards. Rather, he was an unshaven 70-year-old whose physique appeared never to have touched a baseball, much less thrown one.

"I'm Officer Sullivan. Just want to say I was a fan. You were quite a pitcher."

Jack kept his mouth shut.

Sullivan cleared his throat. "My dad talked about you all the time. Well, just thought I'd tell you."

Jack looked down.

"I know it's not much but you could use the bunk. Has to be better than the floor. You gotta be freezing."

Still no reply.

"Take care of yourself. You were one hell of a pitcher," Sullivan said. He motioned with his hand to the wall camera.

The door clanged shut.

"Thanks, kid."

Sullivan turned around before the door locked. He opened the slot. Jack hadn't moved. "No problem, see yah."

## Chapter Two

# Minneapolis - 1965

"You going to throw the damn ball or keep it as a trophy, Jew boy?" a freckle- face batter named Billy shouted.

Jack Rakow, a twenty-year-old rookie, was on the mound for the Minnesota Twins.

"I'll throw it when I'm good and ready. You ain't going to hit it anyway," Jack said.

The umpire called time and took four steps toward the mound. "Son, we have to keep the game going. Throw the fucking ball." He put his mask back on and leaned over the squatting catcher. "Play ball."

Jack stared at the target and the signals the catcher gave: one finger for a fastball, two, a curve, three, slider, four, five. He had no idea what 4 and 5 were. He only had two pitches, a fastball and curve. The catcher flashed his hand again. What the hell? He wound up and threw his curve. Billy swung wildly and missed. So did the catcher. The umpire wasn't as lucky.

The man behind the plate tore off his mask and hopped around the batter's box. A chorus of boos rose from the crowd. "Shit, what's wrong with you?" the ump yelled.

Jack wasn't sure if the question was directed at him or his catcher. Just in case, he shrugged and went back to the mound. His catcher joined him, "They told me you're a—a bit nuts, but now you're pissing off the ump. That's no good."

Jack moved his glove hand to his hip.

"Stop blowing off my signals."

"I will until you get it right. I only throw two pitches," Jack said.

The catcher covered his mouth with his glove. "Fuck it. Throw whatever the hell you want."

The catcher had no idea how crazy he was, and the miracle it took for him to be there. Jack was born in 1945 and together with his parents had survived the charred remains of his father's native Poland. The frustrated catcher and loudmouth batter were nothing.

Jack stood on the mound and drew a breath. He wound up by pivoting on his right leg and extended his right arm behind his shoulder. His left leg was high off the ground as he whipped his arm and body toward the plate. The ball exploded out of his hand. Billy swung. Jack heard a crack. The ball went to first and pieces of the bat flew to third. Jack raced to cover the bag. Billy was called out. He had taken only four steps. He stared at Jack for a moment and then trotted back to his dugout. Jack stood on the mound and rubbed the ball. He'd seen that look a thousand times.

Jack looked around the field. The grass was manicured. The dirt groomed. Fans had come to watch him pitch. He pawed at the ground in front of the rubber. Talk around baseball was his pitches came in so fast the red seams looked like they were on fire. Well, if that's what hitters thought, the better for him. He grinned into his glove and gave the sports buffs what they came to see.

## Chapter Three

# Warsaw, Poland - 1937

Pyotr Rakowski strode into the lecture hall at the University of Warsaw. At six feet tall with a full head of blond hair, his presence was noticed. He looked every inch a Pole. Few knew that underneath his brown tweed suit he kept the covenant of Abraham. He smiled at the small group of students. He was about to start his lecture on "Today's topic: Chopin and Franz Liszt."

"*Dzień dobry*, good morning. Nearly a hundred years ago, Fryderyk Chopin began his career at this University." He stopped speaking to let those words sink in. "He may have sat in this very room." He pointed to a spot in the third row. "Or perhaps, he sat in front near the piano."

The students' eyes widened.

Rakowski glanced at his notes. When he looked up, the door of the lecture hall opened and a young lady walked toward him.

"*Szanowny Panie Profesorze*, Professor Rakowski, you must come with me. There is a telephone for you."

He looked down at his paper and frowned. When he looked up, the girl was only a foot away. The corner of her mouth twitched and her face was pale. Had he been discovered? Was it bad news?

He stared and fought to appear outwardly calm. He saw

6

her mouth move, but the words didn't reach him. She gestured for him to follow. He moved away from his rostrum.

"Excuse me," he said to the class, "I'll return as soon as I can." He bowed his head and followed the girl out.

The heels of his brown leather shoes clacked on the immaculate marble hallway as they hurried to Doktor Jazinski's office. He thought of asking whether she knew what this was all about, but he suspected she wouldn't say.

They climbed three flights of stairs and entered a carpeted hallway that led to the department's chairman's office. The girl opened the floor-to-ceiling door, and held it for him. "Doktor Jazinski is waiting," she said.

"*Dziękuję*, thank you." He stepped through the door and lifted his hand to straighten his tie.

Jazinski was behind his desk the phone to his ear. "Dah," he said and motioned Rakowski over. He covered the speaker and said, "The Foreign Office wants a word with you." He handed him the phone.

Rakowski took it and raised the receiver to his ear. "Yah?"

A bored male voice spoke. "Doktor Rakowski, the Foreign Minister would like to meet with you. Would later this morning be convenient?"

Although he asked it as a question, Rakowski knew it was an order. "Of course," Rakowski said. "Józef Beck wants to meet with me?"

"Please be at the ministry at 11:00 a.m. and ask for his minister's secretary. You will be directed from there. Thank you."

There was a loud click. He had been disconnected. Rakowski handed the phone to Jazinski, who hung it in its cradle.

"The foreign office wants to see me," Pyotr said. "Why? I teach music—Chopin. What could they want from me?"

"I'm sure it is nothing," Jazinski said, his voice betraying his worry. "I'll send Helina to inform your class you will not be returning this morning." He looked down at the papers in front of him. "Professor, you have done good work here…" He let out a sigh. "But, General Pilsudski is dead and in the two years since his passing, Poland has changed and not for the better. Good work is no longer enough." He stood up. "Good luck."

"Thank you, sir. You make it sound like a finality."

Jazinski came around from his desk and placed a hand on his arm. "No, no, you have intellect and charm. Your position is safe as long as I'm here."

A silence settled over the room, but for the ticking of a clock. After several seconds, Jazinski cleared his throat. "I heard you recently became a father. Did you have a boy or a girl?

"A boy—Franciszek Fryderyk, Chopin."

"That's very nice, but it is a mouthful. Yes?"

"To tell you the truth, I just call him Yak or Yakub because of his cheeks. He's three weeks old."

Jazinski looked past him. "Yacub, hmm?"

"That's my nickname for him."

"Yes, I see. Congratulations."

Rakowski nodded and left the office. He had the feeling he had made a mistake.

*Chapter Four*

# 2015 - Chicago

"All right, ladies, Billy Dee is going home now. Better not give my replacement O.B. no trouble. I'll hear about it if you do. Y'all have any questions?" Billy Dee banged on two or three of the cell doors to make sure everyone heard. He walked down the rows until he came to Cell 14. "Hey, Rakow, you still breathing? Don't go do something stupid like kill yourself. That wouldn't be good for the both of us. You'd be dead, but man I'd be left with a mountain of paperwork. The white shirts would be all after me with dumbass questions and in the end my ass will be out on the street. Forty years gone. So, you better be a man about this." He didn't hear a response. "Shit." He opened the slot.

Rakow was curled on the floor next to the toilet.

"You gotta be freezing," Billy Dee said.

Rakow stirred and sat up. He rubbed his arms and legs. "A little."

"Can't do anything for you. Wish I could, but blankets can be used for other things besides keeping warm."

Rakow stood, using the wall to balance himself. It took a few seconds to take several steps toward the door. "Not asking for anything. I just want to know how long I'll be here?"

"Can't say. The dicks must be running around getting

9

what they need. I noticed the Fed cocksuckers are also involved. Those sons-of–bitches can do anything. Have you called anyone in your family?"

He shook his head. "Nah. They don't need to know."

Billy Dee shrugged. "Have it your way, but let me tell you, I'd call someone. Move a little closer to the door, Rakow." Billy Dee lowered his voice. "You didn't hear it from me but your shit ain't goin' away. N-o-o way. Dey want to make an example of you, you know, bein' a celebrity and all that. You goin' to be fucked every which way to Sunday. Get yourself a lawyer. This ain't no damn baseball game."

Rakow blinked. "I suppose you're right. Thanks for the advice." He moved to the far end of the cell and slid down the back wall until he was again sitting on the cold cement floor. "Don't worry, I'm not going to do anything stupid. Not my nature. I've been through worse."

Billy Dee sighed. "Whatever, Rakow, I'll see you in the morning." He closed the slot. It made a loud click when it shut.

*** 

Rakow stared at the heavy metal door. There wasn't much more to see. The walls of his cell were cement blocks painted beige. A fluorescent light hung beneath a drop ceiling and never varied in its brightness. Constant daylight—like Las Vegas without the pizzazz. The *ding, ding, dings* weren't slot machines. They were cell doors opening or closing.

"Yo, Rakow." A man's voice seeped through the wall near his bunk. "Hey, I heard what old Billy Dee was sayin'."

*Shit, not only are the cells freezing, but the walls are thin.* "Yeah? We didn't have a conversation," Rakow said.

"Don't fuck with me. What about you and baseball?"

Rakow sat up. "It ain't your business."

"Hold on, man, I've heard of you. Rakow, you Jack Rakow?"

Rakow rubbed his face. This asshole could be going on all night. "Yeah, that's right."

"You were a pitcher for… Jesus what the fuck was the team… Twins. It was the Twins. My old man was at that game. Said it was the most fucked-up thing he ever seen. You struck out Mantle, Maris, and Howard with the bases loaded. It's about the only thing my old man talked about."

Rakow didn't move. His hands dangled between his knees. The memory brought a smile.

"Yo, you there?"

He couldn't resist. He moved toward the bunk. "Yeah, that…that was me. I walked the first three Yankees. Let's see, the first guy up that inning was the pitcher. Walked him on four pitches. Then Bobby Richardson came up. Out of the five balls I threw, only one was a strike. Kubeck followed. Didn't take his bat off his shoulder. Mickey came next. He was in the batter's box before Kubeck touched first. The crowd went wild. They wanted to tear me limb from limb." *I can still see the smile on Mickey's face*, Jack thought. But aloud he said, "Three pitches later, Mickey went back to the dugout."

"Shit, my old man was sellin' peanuts or some shit. Said he stood in the aisle and didn't move. He couldn't believe it."

"Neither did I."

There was a pause. Rakow put his ear to the wall. "You there?"

"Uh huh. What you in for?"

Rakow moved away. The metal bunk felt colder than the floor. He rubbed his face with his hands. "Who are you?" he asked.

"Tydell Mason. *The man* said I stuck up a couple of grocery stores or some shit. Never did, wasn't there, no how."

"That's good. Hope it works out."

"Come on man…what they got you for?"

He gazed around the room and then leaned against the wall. "A lot of bad shit."

*Chapter Five*

# Warsaw, Poland - 1937

"What has happened to Poland? In the two years since our first President Józef Piłsudski's death, Germany nibbles at Danzig, and the Russians bare their claws. It is Poland's unfortunate geographical luck…" The aide to Foreign Minister Beck put his china cup down haphazardly and missed the saucer. He was short, stocky, built like a bulldog, but his fingers were slender. He eyed Pyotr Rakowski with his dark, almost beady looking eyes. "What should we do?"

"Well, *Pan*, Mr., eh…" Rakowski cleared his throat.

"Kuda Rudolph is my name. I apologize if I hadn't introduced myself. You were saying?"

Rakowski hadn't touched his coffee. He imagined if he reached for the cup, the liquid would spill from his shaking fingers. Instead, he gripped the gold armrest of the chair and sank into the floral upholstery. "I am a professor of music by training. I know little of foreign policy. But in music there are rules, and when the rules are not followed, there is no music."

Kuda reached over and picked up his cup. "I must confess, this is from Vienna. Delicious. The Austrians know about coffee. But you haven't touched yours. Would you like tea instead?"

"No, no, this is fine."

"Ach, I am a bad host. You must be waiting for cake or chocolates. I will ring for them."

"Really, don't bother. I'm just, well, wondering why I'm here."

"Nothing to worry about. I'll ring for some sweets—goes with the coffee."

Kuda pressed a button on the floor. In seconds, there was a knock on the door. A man dressed in a formal frock coat entered.

Kuda spoke to him in German. "Please serve the black forest sacher torte and cookies."

The man nodded and left.

While Kuda ordered, Rakowski took in his surroundings. The room was large, with historical murals of the Battle of Vienna painted on the high vaulted ceiling. They sat on Louis XIV chairs on either side of a roaring fireplace. Side tables with black lacquer tops were beside them. A carved wooden coffee table rested on an intricate Oriental rug. A leather couch sat behind the table several feet from the fire.

"Where were we?" Kuda asked. "Music, politics, and rules, correct?"

"More or less," Rakowski said.

Kuda leaned forward. "Now, my dear professor, in music and politics, what group of people seemed always to break the rules?"

Rakowski pressed the arm of the chair. "I don't know?"

"Come, come, you've studied. Your reputation is superb. You think that American...Gershwin with his 'Rhapsody in...in...'"

"Blue."

"What?" Kuda asked, his face reddened.

"'Rhapsody in Blue.' It's the name of the piece."

Kuda smiled after a second or two. "Yes, of course. What

would you call that piece? Classical like Chopin, or some sort of noise that hurts your head?"

"Well, Pan Kuda, musically speaking, Gershwin is considered a great—"

"No, you miss the point, Dr. Rakowski. That Jew didn't abide by the rules. He invented new ones. That's what I'm saying. Unlike everyone else, the Jews change the rules when they don't like them. Or they invent new ones."

A side door opened and the same man reappeared carrying a silver tray laden with cakes and sweets. He placed it on the table and bowed slightly. "Will there be anything else?"

Kuda waved his hand, a signal for him to leave. "The help should not be seen or heard." He reached for the German black forest cake and took a forkful in his mouth. "The Nazis aren't all bad, you know… Delicious. They've cleaned up their country and made it strong. To tell you the truth… off the record, of course, it wouldn't be a terrible thing if Poland did the same."

*God in heaven.* Rakowski had to remain polite. He reached for a chocolate cookie.

"See, Professor, the pastry is irresistible. It is flown in from Berlin."

Rakowski took a bite. "Yah, I agree."

"Good." Kuda leaned forward and put his hand on Rakowski's knee. "The Foreign Minister has invited you to go to Berlin and attend a conference."

"What kind of conference?"

"Oh, Doktor, there will be lots of your kind there."

Rakowski gripped his chair, but managed to smile. "What do you mean?"

"Professors, thinkers, people from commerce."

"To discuss what?"

"The Jewish Problem."

## Chapter Six

# Minneapolis - 1965

The *Minneapolis Star Tribune* blared, "Only a Hubert Humphrey campaign rally can be compared to this seventh game of the World Series. The crowd will be as large inside the stadium as out."

Jack Rakow tossed the newspaper aside. This was his day. He earned the spot to start this game. He was a shoo-in for Rookie of the Year, or so he had heard. He'd won over twenty games and lost five. That didn't include the third game of the Series. Losing never sat well with Jack…that one in particular. He told himself he should have won, but it seemed the Dodger players always knew what he was about to throw. Now he reached for a cigarette.

"Jack, what time is it?" Her voice from the hotel bedroom pierced the quiet.

He'd forgotten how long he'd been sitting at the table. He checked his watch: 3:00 a.m. Shit. He turned around. He didn't recall who she was. He brushed his hand through his hair. He did remember he and his teammates had gone to a bar. It must have been around nine or ten in the evening. They got him beers and after a while the bartender didn't care he was underage. Someone introduced her… They drank…must have been shots. He remembered looking around and realized everyone else had left.

"Jack?"

She stood in the doorway with a sheet draped around her. "Don't you want any more?" She slowly slid the linen down her shoulders. Her skin was white. He knew its softness. He watched the sheet glide down her body. It revealed her rounded breasts, and then her mid-section and her waist. "Well?" she asked.

He didn't move. "Keep going."

She gave a little laugh. "Okay, if this gets you off." She turned her back to him. The sheet inched down her hips to the top of her ass as she did a little dance.

He didn't make a conscious decision to move from the chair to her. It was more like a magnetic pull.

\*\*\*

He heard a sound. At first it gnawed at the fringes of his sleep. The sound got louder as he awoke. He identified the clamor and sat up in bed. Someone was pounding on the door. He looked over and the girl was asleep next to him. Holy shit. He grabbed his pants from the floor and raced out of the bedroom. He didn't quite close the door.

"I know you're in there. You good-for-nothing sonofabitch," a voice shouted on the other side of the door. "That's my sixteen-year-old daughter with you and I'm going to break every bone in both your bodies."

He almost fell over a chair in the living room. He looked back toward the bedroom. Oh shit. Last night, she was sixteen? Couldn't be, she knew much more than he did. Oh, God, what to do? He grabbed the top of the chair. What time was it? 9:00 a.m. Shit. He had to leave and get to the ballpark.

"I tell you, open up. You fuckin' Jew bastard. Think you own the world. Jesus, if you fucked my daughter I'm going to the cops. That's what I'll do."

He stood stock still and listened. Holy shit, he wouldn't do that, would he? He thought he heard the clock in the bedroom ticking. He waited afraid to take a breath. Finally, there was no more knocking or shouting. He heard footsteps going away from his door.

"What the fuck was that about?" she asked.

He spun around and grabbed his chest. "Huh, you scared the crap out of me. I think that was your old man. He said you're only sixteen?" Jack asked. He said a prayer to himself.

"What's the diff? We had a good time. You're pretty good in there." She nodded toward the bedroom.

"Thanks, well, you are too." Crap. What was he doing? The seventh game of the World Series was this afternoon. "Look, I had a great time and all, but I'm pitching today and I should be at the ball park."

She closed in on him and rubbed against him. "Oh what's a few more minutes. It'll be your lucky day."

"Right." Her hands moved up and down his torso and then massaged his crotch. It took a minute or so to break her spell. "Really, I can't. Besides, whoever that was outside the door said he was calling the cops. You have to leave."

She dropped her hands. "Can't I shower?"

"Shower? No, don't you understand? Who are you, anyway?"

"Now I'm hurt. We fucked like little bunnies all night and you don't even know my name?"

He could feel his face flush. "No, sorry. I remember the bar and the drinks." He took a long look. "And of course your body."

She leaned toward him. "Well, fuck you, Jack Rakow. I know everything about you. You've been on my list for a while."

"List?"

"Uh-huh. I love screwing ball players. Thank your team-mates for setting you up."

"Put your clothes on and get out."

She went to the bedroom and dressed. She picked her purse from the coffee table and took her coat off the couch.

"Thanks for a great time," she said at the door. "And Jack, I am only sixteen. Just wait until it makes the papers. See yah."

## Chapter Seven

# Warsaw, Poland - 1937

Grunia Rakowski was a short, not yet plump woman. Her dark curly hair dangled to her shoulders. She had met her husband in *gimnazjum*—high school. It was their love of music that brought them together. She had trained as a concert pianist. It was their dream to one day afford one for their home. She thought of that as she put the evening's dishes away and then placed the baby in his crib. She sang as many lullabies as she could remember, but it took thirty minutes before he stopped fussing and fell asleep. She closed the door to their bedroom and walked a few steps into their small living room where Pyotr sat.

"Are you sick?" she asked. "You didn't eat much of your dinner."

He didn't look up from his newspaper. "I wasn't hungry."

"Did I do something wrong? It's not easy to cook and clean and take care of our child. Was it the food?"

"No, the food was fine."

"You are not acting yourself, Pyotr. You didn't even hold Yacub."

He threw the paper down. "His name is Fryderyk. Listen. Do not, Grunia, ever call him Yakub. Ever."

Her face paled. "What has gotten into you? Yacub is our

son. That is his name. In this house we swore we would call him Yacub."

"I know what we said." He leaned forward. His voice was taut. "If you want him to survive, use his Polish name and forget about Yacub. Pilsudski is dead and Poland is different now."

"What are you talking? It's just a few crazies. Anti-Semitism is in the past. Our government would not dare dishonor General Pilsudski so soon after his death."

He gazed into her face. *Should I tell her?*

"Pyotr, you are such a pessimist. No one cares that we are Jewish. Our neighbors consider us as Poles."

His consideration for her turned to anger. "I was called to the Foreign Office this morning. I met with a real *grubbamensch*." He had an embarrassed smile. "I mean a swine… a *Pan* Kuda. He's an assistant to Foreign Minister Józef Beck."

"You were at the Foreign Office? You didn't say. Pyotr." She put her hands to her face.

"It wasn't by choice. Someone called the University. We had an interesting conversation."

"My Pyotr met with Józef Beck?"

"No, Grunia, you're not listening. I was with his assistant *Pan* Kuda." Pyotr stood and paced between his chair and the entrance to the kitchen. "Kuda believes the Nazis are doing a wonderful job regarding the Jews."

Grunia put her hand on the top of the other chair. "Pyotr, stop. I don't want to hear. You're frightening me."

"He wants, I should say, he ordered me to go to Berlin."

"Berlin? Germany?" She held onto the side and fell into the seat.

"He wants me to attend a conference on the Jewish Question and report on the effects of Nazi policies on the Jews."

Grunia's eyes widened.

"He thinks Poland should follow Germany. It would keep

our German neighbor happy, and put an end to the Jewish issue in Poland."

"Pyotr, I can't believe…" Tears dripped down her face. "Pyotr, you're not, you can't…"

"What am I to do?" He reached for her hand. "Grunia, where are we to go? There is no place to hide. If I refuse, the University will throw me out."

"No, it is not so. Doktor Jazinski would never…"

He shook his head. "Poland has changed, Grunia. That's what I'm telling you. He'd be forced to."

"When would you leave?"

"Tomorrow morning. I'm to report."

Grunia sat very still. Her mouth made little movements but there were no words. She stared into her hands and then at Pyotr. "*Got in himl*, why are we so cursed? What have we done to deserve this?"

***

"I want to go with you," Grunia said. "Please, Pyotr. I will get my sister to watch Ya— I mean Fryderyk."

Pyotr was still in his undershirt. His brown leather valise was on the bed. He could hear raindrops pelt the one window in the bedroom. It was morning, although it was as dark as night outside. He tuned his wife out and gazed at his small shabby dresser. He didn't know how long he would be gone—a few days, weeks? Damn. He grabbed several pairs of socks and underwear and threw them into the suitcase. He reached for his three white shirts and folded them carefully.

His wife interrupted his concentration. "They'll wrinkle," she said.

He looked up. He hesitated to respond, but gave in. "What can I do?" He then took his only two pairs of pants and folded them too. "I know." His voice rose. He turned toward her. "You want to go with me? Why? You think you'd persuade them not to send me? Look around, Grunia. We Jews have spent a nice ten years, but our Jewish-Polish history is catching up."

"Pyotr, I want to go. It's my place to see you off."

He grabbed her wrists. "This is not the movies. You are not some Hollywood star. Besides, I'm sure they'll be watching. You'll be followed. This trip is enough of a problem."

"You're hurting me. Let go."

She wiped her eyes with the back of her hand and then pulled the edges of her robe closer. "Where will you be staying? How do I reach you?" She let seconds of silence go by.

He took a deep breath. "*Pan* Kuda is meeting me at the station with the train tickets and hotel information. I will call when I arrive in Berlin. It's about a ten-hour trip. If everything goes well."

She turned away. She picked up the baby from the cradle that was next to their bed. "Say good-bye to your father," she cooed. "Your dada is leaving."

Pyotr looked at his son. The baby's eyes opened wide. He stretched his little body and made a *keh* sound.

*A baby's smile always chases away the gloom.* Pyotr smiled back. "You be a good boy, Fryderyk. Don't keep your mother up all hours of the night. You understand?" He then said softly in Yiddish, "*Meyn kind*, my child."

The moment of happiness faded as he grabbed an old belt from the closet to tie the suitcase. Then he looked at his watch. "It's getting late. I don't want *Pan* Kuda to worry I made other plans. Grunia, I'll bring you good German strudel and other treats."

"What will you do there?"

He finished dressing in the tweed jacket he'd worn yesterday. "I'll tell him what I'm sure he already knows. He wants me to be his witness."

"What a terrible man. And you will do this thing?"

He stared at her. She looked angry and scared at the same time.

She covered her mouth with her hand.

"I'm going now," he said.

She put the baby in the crib. "Pyotr, I'm sorry. I'm worried." She went to him and wrapped her arms around him.

He kissed her, then picked up his suitcase. He opened the door and walked down the three flights of stairs. He didn't trust himself to look back.

✳✳✳

The rain splattered his hat and drenched his coat. He took a trolley to the main station on Jerozolimskie Avenue. It was a formidable looking building of heavy brick and cathedral-like spires. *Pan* Kuda and two other men stood at the main entrance.

"*Dzień dobry*," *Pan* Kuda said. "It's good Polish weather to travel." He took a silver flask out of his pocket and had a drink. "You want?"

"That's okay, it's a little early for me."

One of Kuda's men took Pyotr's suitcase as they entered the station.

Inside, Kuda took another swallow and then laughed. "Never too early, Dr. Rakowski." He shoved the flask into his coat pocket. He took Rakowski by his elbow and led him to a dim corner of the main floor. He reached into his suit jacket and withdrew an envelope. "There are 100 Reichsmarks, your passport, train tickets, and hotel reservations. Tomorrow, you are to go to Berlin University and meet with Dr. Reinhart Gertz. He will direct you in your research. We'll meet here in two weeks, same time." He handed the envelope over.

Rakowski took it but didn't put it in his pocket. He tried to be emotionless, but failed.

"You look unhappy," Kuda said. "You are doing your country a great service. The sooner we get a handle on our Jews, the better Poland will be. I will leave you in the hands of my assistants Pawel and Jan. They will show you to the gate. *Dobrą podróż,* have a good trip."

Rakowski thanked him for his wishes and waited for his two guards who waited steps away to escort him.

*Chapter Eight*

# Minneapolis - 1965

Jack double-locked and chained the door before he took a shower. Twenty minutes later, he was downstairs in the lobby of the hotel. He had donned a cowboy hat and sunglasses. He looked around the entrance, which was laid out near the front desk. Several couples and an elderly man were sitting on chairs. A few kids ran around the furniture. No one asked for an autograph. To his relief, there was no crazy father, daughter, or cops waiting for him. He stepped outside and searched for the team bus. He was either early or very late. No one from the team was around. He checked his watch and backtracked through the sliding doors. The bell captain must have seen through the disguise.

"Yeah," he said, "that big old bus pulled out about a minute before you got here."

Jack was stunned. And then he was pissed. "How could they have done that? What has gotten into the boss?"

"Don't worry, kid, I'll get you a taxi. You guys gotta beat those bum Dodgers today." The bell captain's nametag read Ike.

Jack's frustration dissipated. "Thanks. That's exactly what I intend to do. Beat those bums."

Ike's face lit up. "I like that talk, kid." He went outside to flag down a cab.

✳✳✳

The ballpark was about ten miles from downtown Minneapolis. The cab driver made it seem a lot longer. He wouldn't stop talking.

"You gettin' to the ball park kinda early. Well, maybe you'll get some ballplayers to sign something for you. But I tell you those guys playin' today ain't what they use to be. Koufax ain't all that somethin', and Drysdale is a bum. Now Carl Hubbell, there was a pitcher. You ever see him pitch?"

Jack looked at him. "Hey, I'm only twenty. Hubbell was long gone."

The driver stared into the rearview mirror. "What do you know? You're just a kid."

The driver made a left and merged onto the highway. It took a few seconds before he started again. "Bob Feller could throw the ball through Koufax. If the Twins were facing Feller, I'd be worried, but Koufax, ha, a walk in the park. Maybe it's another Jew holiday and the guy won't pitch. How did the Dodgers let Koufax get away with that?"

"What do you mean?" Jack asked. "What if it was Christmas or Good Friday? Anything wrong with observing the day?"

"Whatta ya talking about? Nobody pitches on them days. It's a holiday."

Jack half shut his eyes and willed time to move faster.

Five minutes later, the stadium came into view. "Let me off at the players' entrance," Jack said. He saw the driver check the rearview mirror again.

"No problem." The cab stopped in front of the players' gate.

Jack jumped out and gave the driver a ten-dollar bill.

"It's only a two-dollar fare," the cabbie said.

"Keep it."

The driver held the bill in his hand. "Hey, kid, now I recognize you. Hope you win. Can you sign it?" He held out the ten.

Jack hesitated, then decided what the hell. He scribbled his name and jogged through the players' door. He walked down a tunnel that led to the clubhouse.

"Hey, look who's here?" Frankie yelled. "Romeo has made his appearance. Only the seventh game of the World fucking Series, and we are now blessed with his presence. How good was she?"

Some of the players moved toward Frank. "Knock it off. Sam will handle it." Big Tony at 6-foot-2 and some 190 pounds silenced everyone. He turned to Jack. "Sam wants to see you, now."

Jack dropped his duffel bag in front of his locker and went down a hall to the manager's office. The door was closed. He knocked.

"It ain't locked," Sam yelled out. "Get your ass in here."

Jack twisted the handle and went in. The pitching and batting coaches sat around a battered wooden desk. The room was thick with cigarette smoke. Sam made a gesture, and the coaches left.

"Sit down," he said.

Jack did.

"This a joke to you?" Sam asked. "You come waltzing in here after missing the team bus. The night before the biggest game in your life, you're out carousing with some underage whore. Who the fuck you think you are? I'd like to trust you, but I can't. Unlike you, this game means a whole lot to me—a lifetime of trying to get to this moment. You ain't pitching. Jim Kaat is starting."

"Wait a minute, you can't—"

"Let me tell you something, kid." Sam leaned over the desk. "I can and I will. One more thing, you'll never pitch for me again. Now get your ass out of here and pray to your fuckin' God that we win."

∗∗∗

Jack slouched at the end of the dugout. The whole team seemed to know what had happened in the manager's office. He was now bad karma and no one would sit near him. To pass the time, he flipped a ball in the air to catch. After a while, he glanced down the bench during the Twins' home half of the first. He didn't want to be obvious. He tried to think who had set him up. Three of them wanted to pitch this game. Two of them were with him at the bar, but the guy who got the start wasn't.

Koufax made fast work of the Twins in their inning at bat. The team took the field for the top of the second. Jim Kaat was on his game too, and the Dodgers were out in no time.

Jack popped gum in his mouth and took another look. Anyone could have been in on it. The backup catcher never liked him. There were probably others. Shit, he always felt he wasn't part of the team even when they celebrated his victories. He studied his glove. He thought of his parents. They were tough people. Brusque, sometimes ill mannered, they had no time for rules. If something couldn't be done one way, they would try another. They were foreigners— survivors of the Holocaust. They thought of themselves as "Greeners" in Yinglish, which was what they called Yiddish mixed with English.

Hell. He was born in a DP—displaced persons—camp, Feldafing, near Munich. Once they moved to America, he was the kid on the block whose mother yelled for him with a strange accent. Her voice could penetrate a stadium of yelling fans. "Yankella, come home." Being teased by the other kids on the block was a part of life.

His attention snapped back to the playing field. He leaned forward. Kaat delivered the first pitch to Lou Johnson for a strike. The second was a ball. "Don't throw a heater," he said to himself. He saw Kaat wind and deliver. Shit, a fastball on the inside of the plate. The sound of the bat striking the ball told him trouble was coming. He tracked the line drive all the way into the outfield seats. Not a good way to start the fourth inning. Dodgers led 1 to 0. He shoveled more gum in his mouth.

The next batter was Ron Fairly who blasted Kaat's first pitch for a double to right. Jack stood. He spotted Al Worthington warming in the bullpen. Kaat was going to have a short afternoon. He took two or three steps toward the pitching coach. The son of a bitch spat out a stream of tobacco juice and turned toward Sam. Jack went back to his seat and pounded his fist into his glove. Wes Parker was next at bat. Kaat's pitch didn't fool him. He hit a single and another run scored. Sam sprinted to the mound and brought in Worthington.

The rest of the game passed quickly despite two more pitching changes. Jack tried to ask God for a miracle, but He was too busy to listen. Two hours and twenty-seven minutes was all it took for Koufax to pitch a nine-inning shutout. Too bad he didn't have another Jewish holiday to observe.

## Chapter Nine

# Warsaw, Poland - 1937

Pyotr said nothing to his two escorts, Pawal and Jan. He stood between them and watched a stream of people hurry to catch their trains. Occasionally, Pyotr's gaze met his guards' eyes, but then he looked away. A small crowd formed around them. He could hear snippets of conversations, women chuckling over something clever. Several men smoked. Pyotr reached into his coat pocket. His two escorts slid their hands toward the inside of their coats. After Pyotr extracted a pack of cigarettes, his guards relaxed and grinned.

"*Amerykański papierosy*, American cigarettes—Camels."

"Da, yes. An uncle of mine sent them. You want?" Pyotr shook out the pack and offered. The two took several and stuffed them in their pockets.

"You can get more?" Pawal asked.

Pyotr shrugged. "Don't know, but when I get back I'll ask."

Pawal slapped him on the back. "You a good Joe."

Pyotr rolled his eyes and thought the man had watched too many *Amerykański* films.

Jan only smiled.

Pyotr looked at his watch. "The train should arrive in about five minutes. I want to buy some newspapers." He pointed to a stand fifty yards away. "It's a long trip. Don't worry, I'll come back."

The two guards exchanged words. "Okay," Pawal said, "we'll wait here."

He came back with several German and Polish newspapers; among them was *Der Stürmer*.

Jan pointed to the German paper. "I read that every day. Streicher understands the Jews well. He knows what to do with them."

Pyotr nodded. "I've heard Herr Streicher, the publisher of the paper, has a large following. I'll need to catch up."

The train pulled into the station. Pyotr's two escorts led him to the third car. The first two were for first and second-class.

"You are travelling in style—third class." Pawal laughed and pushed Pyotr forward. "Here, take. Vodka. It's a long journey." He tossed him an old flask.

"*Dziękuję*, thank you." He climbed the three steps into the car and pushed his way down the aisle. The window seats were all taken. Where did all these people come from? Finally, he saw an aisle seat next to a woman. Another was unoccupied next to a large man with a bow tie.

"*Przepraszam, czy to miejsce jest zajęte?*, Excuse me, is this seat taken?" Pyotr asked.

The woman turned from the window. She gave him a quick glance, picked up a box from the seat, and placed it on her lap. Then she looked away.

Pyotr thanked her. There were no porters in third class to help with the valise. He glanced at the shelf above the seats. It was crammed with suitcases.

"Sit," she said, "and put your luggage underneath, like this. It will be easier for you at the border."

He must have looked puzzled.

"The Germans search everyone and everything. They are very thorough, but impatient. The more you are in order, the less trouble you will have."

"Oh." He reached into his pocket for his Camels.

"But." She turned again. He had a full view of her face. Black hair peeked out from under her wide brimmed hat. Her skin color was milky white, and round, dark eyes set off her face. Bright red lipstick outlined her petite mouth.

"But what?" he asked.

Her eyes widened. A small smile played around her lips. She leaned toward him and whispered, "Too much in order, and the bastards will cart you off and hold you for questioning. Your paper, *Der Stürmer,* won't save you. Get rid of it."

Was this a trap? Who was this woman? He thought of the man with the bow tie whose seat he didn't take. Maybe he should have.

Pyotr flicked his lighter several times. He had neglected to completely load it with fluid. His hand shook slightly. He sensed his seatmate was watching. What a fool he was. He stopped and with an embarrassed grin tapped out a cigarette and offered it to her.

She nodded and took it. She fished out matches from her purse and with one strike, lit hers and then his. She inhaled deeply and blew out the smoke. "First time travelling to Berlin?"

He hesitated, then decided to answer. "Yes, I'm going to a conference."

"You will enjoy. Berlin is a beautiful city."

As he drew on his cigarette, a high-pitched whistle sounded. He lurched forward. The air brakes were released and the train began to move. He looked past her through the window and saw the station slide by. Raindrops soon pelted the car.

"So you've been to Berlin?"

"Many times. I am the secretary for Gesellschaft für Musik und Literatur für Czechoslovakia, the Society for Music and Literature for Czechoslovakia. I travel all over Eastern

Europe as well as Paris. It's the people that are ugly and getting uglier."

She reached for his newspaper and held it out. "*Der Stürmer* is filth. Every word of it is a lie, but because it's in print, people accept it as true. Hitler and Goebbels are geniuses in making people believe shit is spun gold."

He glanced around the car. Hopefully no one else heard. "You are certainly opinionated, Pani…"

"Katalyna Paternoskov, and I am not a Mrs. Well, not in the normal sense. I am a free thinker and marriage is not free. Is that not so…Pan?"

He felt a headache coming on. He pinched the bridge of his nose, then rubbed his forehead. "Pyotr. My name is Pyotr Raskowski. I am a professor of music at the University." He remembered the flask of vodka, and became very thirsty. He envisioned a very long trip.

"Very nice to meet you, Pyotr. Your response?"

"You want an answer?" he asked.

Her eyes sparkled and she wore a small smile. "Yes, Professor, I do."

"Marriage is like—breathing. It is what two people do to raise a family. Otherwise, as everyone knows, there would be chaos."

"So marriage is only important if there is a family? What if it is decided that you don't want children. What then?"

His finger traced the outline of the flask in his coat pocket. "Then… I don't know. It's not right and it's never been right. It is the order of things. A man living with a woman must be married. Every religion, Christianity, Judaism, Mohammadism, all follow that principle. It is what God wants."

"Ah hah. So now you bring in God," she said. "When you're stuck for an answer you answer with, it is what God wants." She sighed. "So predictable." Her hands jabbed the air and her voice rose. "God is not involved. God is not looking down from the heavens. God—"

"Pani Paternoskov, I mean, Katalyna, please lower your voice. This is a discussion between us alone, not the entire train."

His rebuke caught her in midpoint. Her hands dropped to her lap.

"No one has…" She looked at him with a mixture of frustration and humor. "Ach, if you don't want to talk, go read your filthy newspaper."

*Thank God*, he thought. *Der Stürmer* may be rot but at least it would be quiet. He unfolded the paper. The headline in German read *Jüdische Verschwörung zum Tod von Nichtjuden: Jewish Plot to kill Gentiles Uncovered.* He felt a knot in his stomach and his mouth went dry. He began to read.

"You must think I am crazy. I can assure you, I am not," she cut in. "I am normal—as normal as one can be in these times. The world has changed."

He wanted to ignore her, to be left alone to digest this evil. Surely, this couldn't be widely read or believed. There had always been crackpots who made wild accusations against the Jews. *The Elders of Zion* was popular during the Russian pogroms in the late 1800s. It accused Jews of drinking non-Jewish children's blood during Passover. Most regarded that as stupid and untrue, but there were others…

He turned towards her. "You were saying about the times?"

She stared back. "The times, dear professor, are not ours."

Something about her voice had changed. There was softness to it, almost wistful. He put the paper to the side. It surprised him to feel relief. In an instant, the ugliness of *Der Stürmer* was pushed aside. "Things haven't changed so much. Our peasants remain our peasants. Their lives are little different than in Wladyslaw Reymont's novel *Chlopi.*"

She smiled. "Of course you would know of Reymont.

The pride of Poland's literature, 1924 Nobel Laureate." Her voice deepened. "Heavy, dry, and religious. Myself, I like George Bernard Shaw. You laugh when he bites. He is much more clever."

The newspaper on his lap slipped to the floor. He bent down but decided to leave it.

She motioned toward it. "You don't want your paper?"

He hesitated. "It belongs there."

Their eyes met. She retrieved it. "It would be bad manners. Better to put it between the seats."

"Can it be true? He pointed to the headline. "Do people really believe this?"

"Oh, professor, open your eyes and ears. The sounds of German marching boots are all around."

"I can't..." He shook his head. He decided to have a drink and took out his flask. He looked over at Katalyna. "You want?"

She glanced at her watch. "It's still morning." Then she shrugged. "Oh, why not?"

"*Na Zdrowie*, cheers," she said as her hands clutched the container and she took a swig. She wiped her mouth with a tissue, then returned the flask.

He took a gulp. The vodka warmed him. He screwed the cap back on, then slipped it into his pocket. He squeezed his eyes shut. The train would be at the border in sixty minutes.

## Chapter Ten

# 2015 - Chicago

Billy Dee Jackson relaxed in his easy chair. His fifty-five-inch Sony was on the other side of his family room. He turned the sound up, then grabbed a beer from the fridge. The Cavaliers had the Bulls on the ropes. Cleveland opened the fourth quarter with a ten-point run and tied the score. He was so into the game that he was startled when his wife, Janine, came and stood in front of the screen.

"Turn that thing down," she said. "I've been trying to tell you there's a call."

"What? Get out of the way. Who is it?"

"It's Flynn, the desk sergeant."

"Shit, what does he want?"

His wife didn't move. "I don't know, best you go find out."

Billy Dee got out of his chair and moved slowly to the kitchen. After a day of work he was in no rush. "Yeah, this is Billy Dee, what's doing, Sarge?" There was static on the line. "Hello?"

"Billy Dee?"

"Yeah, what's going on?"

"Sorry to bother you, but was there a Jack Rakow in lockup when you left?"

"Sure as hell was." Billy Dee tightened his grip on the phone. "What you sayin'? Somethin' happen to him?" Static exploded over the line. "You there, Sarge?" He took the phone from his ear, glanced at it. The connection cleared. "Hello?"

"Yeah…these damn phones. Anyway, I'm looking at the book, and someone wrote Rakow's name and took him. Rakow is gone."

"Gone? Who?"

"That's just it, we don't have any personnel with that star number."

"Let me get this straight. Rakow got signed out by an officer who isn't CPD?"

"That's what it appears to be."

"Lord have mercy. Did you talk to O.B.? He relieved me. He been doin' this for a long time."

"It was the first thing I did. He's in with the captain now. He told me everything was in order."

"Jesus." Beads of sweat formed on Billy Dee's forehead. His wife came into the kitchen.

"What's wrong?"

He waved her away. "Are you on a pax or a bell phone?" he asked.

"Pax," Flynn answered.

"Good. you know the 'G' was nosing around Rakow's case. They could have signed him out."

"Uh-huh, well the 'G' is sending someone here to look at the signature. From the conversation they had with the captain, the 'G' didn't recognize the name."

"Lawd, Lawd, Lawd."

"You better get down here. The Captain wants a word with you."

"I'm sure he do. It'll take me a little bit, but tell him I'm coming."

"See you when you get here, Billy Dee."

He hung up the phone.

"Well?" his wife asked.

"I gots to go down to the station."

"Uh-huh, for what?"

He took his time to answer. He lowered his eyes and stared, which meant *don't stick your nose where it don't belong.* He knew if he said "police business," it would only invite more questions, but he said it anyway.

"Now look here, Billy Dee, I ain't havin' none of this. You tell me straight. What's going on where you have to go traipsin' down to work at this hour of the night?" She planted her hands on her hips.

"Janine, it's nothin' to get all up about. A prisoner been lost. He was an old time baseball player. That's why all the fuss. Probably some fool didn't do the paperwork. Let me get dressed. The sooner I'm gone, the sooner I'll be back."

"You mean like someone lost keys but instead it's a person?"

"I don't like where that's headin'—just got to get to the bottom of it."

"Well, you make sure dat you ain't where the shit falls. I'm lookin' forward to your retirement pension."

"Okay, baby."

\*\*\*

Billy Dee parked his Chrysler 200 in the police lot of Area North at Belmont and Western. Riverview, a large amusement park had been there for decades until the City took over the land and built a police station. The memories of freshly popped corn and the taste of cotton candy always brought a smile. The roller coaster filled with people screaming and laughing as it gathered speed was probably where the back of the station ended. The spirit of the carnival remained. It just moved inside. Billy Dee grabbed his battered leather satchel from the front seat and climbed out. The air seemed colder closer to Lake Michigan than at his home on the South Side. He saw his breath and put on gloves as he walked toward the entrance. His hand was on the door when he heard his name. He turned and saw someone in a parka. The hood covered the face.

"Officer Jackson?"

The voice was female. How the hell did she know his name?

"I'm Melissa Stone."

His eyes narrowed. He didn't recognize the name or, from what he could tell, the person.

She took off her hood and shook out her long, dirty blonde hair. "Damn, it's cold out here."

"I guess so."

"I heard earlier today that Jack Rakow had been arrested."

He took a step back and eyed her with suspicion. "Who did you say you were?"

"Oh, sorry, I'm a reporter from *Sports Magazine,* the online side. I've been waiting out here hoping that you could give me a scoop."

"Don't know what you're talking about or why you'd think I would know."

"You're the lock-up keeper."

How the hell she know that? "Look, Miss. I can't talk. I don't know where you got your information but—"

"You're Billy Dee Jackson. I know you've seen and spoken to Mr. Rakow."

"What?"

"So you're not denying it?" she asked.

"This is bullshit. Lady, I don't know who you are or where you came from. I don't have nothin' to say to you." He started toward the door.

"He's missing."

Billy Dee stopped. "Say that again?"

"Jack Rakow. He's missing. You have a leak inside that building."

"Is that so?" He left her outside and went into the building. The hallway was deserted. Shit. He rubbed his face. This ain't gon' to be good, but this missy knows something. *Sorry, Janine,* he said silently to his wife, *but I got a missing prisoner and…* He went back outside.

He took her arm and guided her toward the parking lot. "Jesus, Lord have mercy, lady, Ms. Stone, whatever, let's talk."

"That's what I wanted all along. Where can we go? The police station may not be the best. Like I said, you have a leak."

He looked at his watch. Shit, the Captain was waiting. He considered what she said and swore to himself. Hell of a fix. "Okay, I'll meet you at Tracy's."

"Where's that?"

"About six or seven blocks west on Belmont."

She blinked. "I'm not familiar with the city."

"Take this street," and pointed in the direction. "If you pass the river, you've gone too far."

"Okay. It will take me awhile."

"Why?"

"I don't have a car."

"You…what? For God's sake." He took a deep breath. This was going from bad to worse. "

*Chapter Eleven*

# Boston - 1975

"Jack, you've been around a long time. You've pitched in a World Series. How does this one compare?"

"Well, Curt, every time you get here, you thank your lucky stars. My first was when I was a rookie with Minnesota. It was a wonderful series and I got to see two of the greats, Jim Kaat and Sandy Koufax. I don't think I realized how lucky I was."

"Do you have any idea on how you're going to pitch to the Big Red Machine, Cincinnati Reds?"

"Carefully."

"That's a good one. Best of luck to you. There you have it, Jack Rakow of the Boston Red Sox."

He shook Curt Gowdy's hand and mouthed a few words off-mike. The TV sports announcer and his cameraman laughed, then went toward the press box. Jack trotted back to the dugout.

El Tiant, Louis Tiant, Boston's number one starter, eyed him as he moved down the steps. "Nice going, Rakow. Hope you'll pitch as good as you talk."

"Better," he said and went to where Tiant sat. "Just give me the ball and you'll see."

El Tiant smiled and spat. "*Sí,* you had your chance. I'm numero uno, today."

Jack looked down to where Tiant's spit landed and then back at him. "It all goes real fast. Enjoy it while you can. Hope your aim is better out there than here." He reached for his glove that was on a shelf and made his way down the bench.

As game time approached, he and the other players assigned to the bullpen left the dugout. He wore his warm-up jacket over his uniform. He gazed at the stands. Every seat was taken. A sea of Boston blue broken up by Cincinnati fans in red. The crowd erupted into cheers as the Red Sox sprinted to their positions on the field. The outfield grass looked greener than it had all season. He took a deep breath. The scoreboard flashed the date: October 11th...Saturday. Hmm...at least God can't be too angry with him. He wasn't pitching on the Sabbath.

It was a crisp day. The kind of weather a pitcher loved. He looked toward the mound and saw Tiant take his warm-ups. If only... He knew he was luckier than most. He was in his tenth year, which to many was a career. His fastball wasn't as fast and his curve not as sharp. He now had a third pitch, a split finger fastball. It came at the batter straight and then dropped. It kept him in the majors.

"Hey, you should do some throwing," Don Bryant, the bullpen coach, said.

"It's a little early. I'm slated for the third game. That's about four days away with the travel day."

"The skip wants to know about your arm. You've been a little off."

He shrugged. "What the hell. Let's wait until after the national anthem. Show respect."

"Whatever you say, Rakow."

Minutes later, the voice over the loudspeaker asked everyone to stand for the singing of "The Star-Spangled Banner." The stadium quieted. At the end of the rendition, the fans roared their approval. Jack grabbed a ball and went to the bullpen pitching rubber.

"Let's see what you got." Bryant crouched behind the plate and raised his glove for a target.

Jack took a breath and as he had done countless times before, wound up and threw. A pain shot down his arm. He bit his lip.

"Was that your fastball?"

He found his voice. "Why? You didn't see it?"

Bryant shook his head. "My grandson can throw harder."

"Then your grandson will have the hitters on their front foot looking stupid when they miss."

The look on Bryant's face told him he didn't buy it. "Throw like you mean it, Rakow."

"Let me get loose. That was the just first pitch."

"Whatever."

He threw several more pitches and the pain lessened. His velocity picked up and his curve was sharp.

"Thatta way, Rakow. Now you're cooking. Give me ten more."

It may have been the day, but he was in rhythm. His motion was fluid and the ball went exactly where he wanted. It was a great day to pitch.

After five minutes, Bryant held up his hand. "Okay, Rakow, save some for the game. I'll tell the Skip you're ready."

He caught the ball from the coach and rolled it around in his glove. He went back to the bench and got his jacket.

"You were humming, Rake," said Dick Pole, one of Boston's relief pitchers. "The Big Red Machine better look out."

"I'll try to give them more than they can handle." He sat down. It didn't take long before he felt pain shoot from his elbow to his hand. He bent forward and cradled his arm across his chest. When he thought no one was looking, he rubbed his forearm. Shit, this was trouble.

He began to sweat. He rolled his eyes. It wasn't even 60 degrees. He shouldn't be sweating—one more game, God, just one more.

"You okay?" Pole asked.

He looked up. "Yeah, yeah." He let his arm drop to his side. "Great day for a ball game, isn't it?"

Pole wiped his forehead under his Boston cap with the back of his hand. "Sure is, but what's with…" He nodded toward Jack's arm.

Jack gaze followed his. He smiled. "Just a sign of age. The arm is telling me I'm no longer twenty."

"Maybe the trainer should look at it?"

"Come on, Dick, that ain't gonna happen. Every pitcher gets a little sore by this time in the season. It's nothing to worry about. I'll be fine."

"So you say, but it's the World Series."

"Think I don't know that?"

Pole took a seat down the bench. Jack searched out the scoreboard. It was 0 to 0 top of the second.

"Excuse me," he heard someone say.

He saw a man in an Andy Frain blue uniform in front of him. What the hell was an usher doing in the bullpen?

"You Jack Rakow?" the usher asked.

Jack nodded.

"I have a telegram for you."

Jack leapt to his feet. "Let me see that." He grabbed the envelope and tore it open. He read the message once, and a second time. "Oh my God."

*** 

The World Series played on three TVs mounted from the ceiling in a lounge at Logan Airport. El Tiante was throwing well. His pitches were going down faster and better then the two scotches Jack already had. His third was on deck. The bartender wiped a spot near his glass.

"Louie is pitching good, huh."

Jack looked at him and then glanced at the screen. He saw the catcher give the sign. "He's going to throw a curve and Joe Morgan is going to whack it." Seconds later, Morgan swung and hit the ball squarely. The camera followed the ball. Curt Gowdy started to yell the drive had home run distance and the game was scoreless. The ball went to the right of the foul pole. The bar noise that had quieted exploded in relief.

"That was close," the bartender said, as if he was describing an incoming missile. "Say, how did you know— Wait a minute. Aren't you... What are you doing here?"

"Emergency back home."

"Sorry, pal—must be rough. Hey, the round is on me. Here's to the Red Sox."

"Thanks—to the Red Sox." Jack gulped the drink and started to cough. "Went down too fast," he sputtered and grabbed a glass of water. People looked in his direction. After a few seconds he regained his voice.

"It's all right," he said and held up his hand. "I'm okay, really." He slid from his seat and dropped a twenty on the bar. "Boston will win," he said, "we've got the players this year." He didn't stay around to discuss it.

His flight to Chicago was out of C-15—the last gate in the terminal. People were crowded around TVs that airport management provided in honor of the Red Sox. In Boston, everyone is a fan. Still, the strangeness of trotting down a cement corridor instead of the dirt and grass of a ball field wasn't lost on him. Going home would be hard enough, but this... He reached C-15 and plopped down in a chair facing the window. Planes bearing the United logo were on either side of his gate. He watched like a kid as planes disengaged from the ramps and rumbled toward the runway. He never got tired of the magic.

Going to the airport with his father had been like a trip to Disneyland. It didn't matter that he was forced to wear a tie and a jacket. To his father this was a formal occasion. For Jack, the noise of the propellers and the crowds of people waiting made up for the enforced dress code.

"Come on, Yankeleh, " his father would say, "The plane is here." They would race down the corridors of Midway Airport. Their gate was always the last one. His dad walked fast; he had to run to keep up. His father was tall with long legs, but he was a little boy. It must have been a sight. At the gate, he dodged and wiggled his way to the front and waited by the ramp door. After what seemed like a long time, he heard the whine of an engine and then moments later, a click. The door opened. People streamed through. His aunt from Toronto was a tiny woman who was easy to miss. He kept his eyes peeled. Within minutes, everyone seemed to have exited the plane. The crowd thinned.

He saw his dad take a step or two. His father had a big smile. Yankeleh turned toward the door. There she was—his only aunt, Dvorah. She was all smiles despite her heart problems and the past. She didn't have to sweep him up in her arms; they were almost the same height.

"So how's by you?" his father asked.

"Good," she replied.

He came to learn that bad was over there, in Europe, where everything had been lost. It was always good, here.

Jack rubbed his face. It wasn't that many years ago. Now his father was in the hospital, and he was coming home.

## Chapter Twelve

# Warsaw, Poland - 1937

Katalyna told Pyotr she was hungry and to join her in the dining car. It took him five minutes to decide. Was he crossing a moral boundary lunching with a woman, particularly one as outspoken and free as she was? He was married, for God's sake, a father. He took a puff on his cigarette. What could be so wrong? It was lunch, a meal. He needed to eat. *Ach*. He should have brought a sandwich like his wife suggested. He checked his pockets. He had 10 zlotys and *RM*100 in marks. It ought to be enough for the trip. He got up and straightened his tie and jacket. He held onto the leather straps that ran the length of the car and made his way.

She sat at a table with another couple. He hesitated, but she waved him over.

"These people invited us to sit with them. I left a place for you," she said. "This is Herr Farber and Frau Bauer. They are travelling to Paris with a stop in Berlin. "

"Pleased to meet you," Pyotr said. He sat and placed the white linen napkin on his lap.

"Frau Paternoskov told us you are a professor of music at the University," Herr Farber said.

"Yes, my specialty is Chopin."

"*Hmm*, Chopin."

"Something wrong?"

"No, Herr Professor, only his music cannot be compared to a Beethoven or Mozart." He spread his hands over the table.

"I don't understand."

"Besides, how is that a specialty? You either play him or listen to others. Is that not so, Frau Bauer?" He laughed.

"You are so witty, Martin, oops, I mean, Herr Farber. His specialty is then a player, like a *kartenspieler,* a card player, yes?" She batted her eyes and brushed her blonde curls away from her face.

Herr Farber's face reddened. He glared at his companion and then his face dissolved into a smile. "That is funny. A kartenspieler of Chopin. Oh, that is too good." He squeezed her hand.

"I'm sorry, what is the humor?" Pyotr asked.

Katalyna rushed in. "He takes music very seriously. Let's order. The waiter is here."

"Yes, good idea," Herr Farber said. He looked at his watch and then the menu. "Luncheon, the Bavarian Weisswurst and Pretzel look delicious." He turned to Frau Bauer. "For you?"

"I'll have…" She twiddled a spoon. "…liver dumpling soup and then the pork roast with spätzle." She licked her lips. "Oh, and a beer."

"So much food for someone as petite as you. Where do you put it?" Herr Farber asked.

She blushed. "I use a lot of energy."

"Sports?" Pyotr asked.

"Umm, in a fashion. Right, Mar… Herr Farber?"

Farber's gaze went around the table. His hands then went to his shirt collar to fix his already straight tie. "Yes, sports, she's an international tennis player," he said.

"Like I'm a *kartenspieler,*" Pyotr said under his breath.

Katalyna shot him a look. Then she announced she would

have a schnitzel along with a glass of moselblümchen. "And you, Herr Docktor?" she asked Pyotr.

He studied the menu. Almost everything on it had pork. He gazed over the leather-bound bill of fare. Everyone seemed to be watching. He wasn't an observant Jew, but pork was a line he wouldn't cross. "I'll have a kaffee and apple strudel."

"Come, come, Herr Professor, at least have some soup," Herr Farber said.

Pyotr held up his hand. "No, it is enough. I lost my appetite with all this sitting."

Herr Farber went on as if he didn't hear. "Professor, soup shows the German in us. I find it a patriotic duty that the main course be something German."

The whoosh of a passing train and the *click-clack* of the wheels drowned out the table's conversation. "What was that?" Pyotr asked.

Farber repeated his remark.

Pyotr used his napkin to wipe his mouth. "Herr Farber, I commend you. If our patriotism were limited to food, we would grow fat, happy, and be at peace. I am Polish, but to acknowledge the excellent German cuisine, I ordered the strudel."

Farber continued the argument. "*Der Strudel ist nicht zufriedenstellend. Es ist nur Nachtisch.* The strudel is not satisfactory. It is only dessert." He motioned to the waiter. "A schnitzel for the professor."

Katalyna must have seen Pyotr's eyes register panic. She took a breath and reached for her wine. "A toast to German food. It's delicious, hearty, and may it be enjoyed for years to come." She held her glass out.

Farber hesitated, and then shook his head. "*Yah, um deutsche Küche.* To German food," and clicked his glass to hers.

Pyotr and Frau Bauer joined in.

"You know, Herr Farber," Katalyna continued, "such food can be appreciated without eating. I am sure the Professor respects the preparation of these tasty dishes." She then smiled. "You don't have to be a player of Beethoven to love his music."

Farber still had his wine glass raised. "Such charm and wit. You are a fortunate man, Professor."

Pyotr nodded. "She is as delightful as Frau Bauer."

Farber looked over at his companion. "Yah," he said, and sipped his wine loudly.

## Chapter Thirteen

# 2015 - Chicago

Billy Dee drove out of the police lot. Neither he nor his passenger, the sports reporter Melissa Stone, talked. He wanted to think. Who the hell would be that stupid to leak, and more important, why? He glanced at the half-smoked cigar resting in his ashtray. Damn, he could use a smoke. He looked over at Melissa.

"I prefer Romeo and Julieta, myself," she said. "The smoke is smoother and more tasteful, particularly the maduro."

"Huh?" Billy Dee's hand stopped in midair.

"Cigars. You're smoking…"

"A Mac."

"Oh, you like Macanudos."

"Jesus, yeah, it's a Macanudo." He lit it and drew.

"Smells great," she said. "I'll join you if you have another."

He took another puff, and hit the accelerator. *Who is this broad?* He saw the sign for the bar half a block away. This may not have been his best idea. Too late. He checked his upper pocket. "Sorry, don't have one."

She appeared disappointed.

Good. "Look," he said, "I'm not trying to be a friend or your buddy. You said there's a leak."

"Come on now, Officer Jackson, you've driven me to a

bar. The least you can do is buy me a drink. I was out there awhile waiting for you."

"Okay, okay, I get it. One drink and then you'll tell me."

"Sure. God only knows what I'd say after two."

He drew on the cigar and then exhaled. The smoke filled the car. Instead of gasping, Melissa took a deep breath. "My dad was a cigar smoker. I guess I get it from him."

"Yeah?"

"Any chance he got, he would light one."

"No kidding."

"The smell reminds me of him."

"Is he still…"

"No. He passed away two years ago."

"Sorry." Billy Dee glanced at his cigar. "And your mom let him smoke?"

She gave him a look. "What do you think?"

"Got it," he chuckled. Yeah, that was usually the way. He put the cigar back in the ashtray. "Okay, let's have that drink."

They walked by two people at the bar hunched over, clutching their glasses. A basketball game played on an old TV resting on a shelf above them.

"To the back," Billy Dee said.

There were five empty tables. "Grab a seat."

She looked at her choices. "It may be better to stand. Those stools look like they've been through war, and not on the winning side."

"Suit yourself. What are you drinking?"

"Vodka tonic. Grey Goose."

He gave her a look. "You'll be lucky they have Smirnoff's."

She shrugged. "Then whatever."

He ordered her drink and a beer for himself. Bud or Miller were the house brands, usually the only brands. On occasion, Pat the bartender had Old Style, but not tonight. He brought the drinks back to the table.

She took a sip.

"I've done my part," he said.

"Geez, won't you let a girl enjoy her drink?"

"Not so loud."

She looked around. "There's no one here besides the two up front. I think they have other things on their minds."

"I shouldn't even be in this damn place, and certainly not with someone like you. I mean a reporter, or whatever you are."

"I'm a sports reporter, like I told you. I've been working on the Jack Rakow story."

"Really?"

She leaned closer. "For months."

"You've been working on this guy's story that long?" Billy Dee asked. "Why? He's been out of baseball for, what, thirty, thirty-five years. What's newsworthy about Jack Rakow?"

Melissa finished her drink. "How about another? On me."

He jiggled his almost empty can of beer. "Sure."

She walked over to the bar. Billy Dee couldn't help staring at her ass. *Mercy.* He emptied the can.

She came back and put the drinks on the table. "An Old Style for you, and Grey Goose for me. Pat said he kept the good stuff for special occasions."

He gave her a look and popped the top.

"Actually, it's the fortieth anniversary of the 1975 World Series between Boston and Cincinnati," she said.

"So?"

"Rakow went to Chicago during the first game. His father was sick or something.

"Yeah?"

"Do you remember the series?" she asked.

"Kind of. That's when Boston's catcher… Shit, what was his name? He played for the White Sox later on…"

"Carlton Fisk."

"That's right." Billy Dee closed his eyes for a second, then opened them. "I can picture Fisk going toward first, waving his arms willing that ball fair. He was a son of a bitch."

"You're right about that," and took a sip.

"Okay, so what does any of this have to do with anything,"

"Well, Officer Jackson, our friend Jack Rakow never pitched a game in that series."

He stared at her, his hand on his beer. Maybe he didn't hear or he missed something she said. His wife constantly accused him of not listening. He took a long pull and set the can down. He leaned toward her. "What am I missing? So Jack Rakow didn't pitch in the 1975 World Series. I probably knew that and forgot. So what."

She didn't have much left of her drink. She lifted her glass, tilted her head, and finished it off. She smacked the glass on the table. "You know why he didn't pitch a game?"

"No, but you're about to tell me."

She smiled. "Very good." She lowered her voice. "He didn't come back."

*Chapter Fourteen*

# Warsaw, Poland - 1937

Pyotr left his lunch companions before the meal ended. He knew what etiquette required. He had listened to Herr Farber and his blonde friend insist it was the duty of every German to right the wrongs inflicted upon the *Vaterland*. In between mouthfuls of sausage, Herr Farber would expand on the virtuous of the German people and German culture. The conversation grew insufferable. There wasn't much left of Pyotr's tongue to bite. So he folded his napkin and placed it on the table.

"I'm so sorry," he said, "but the motion of the train and the coffee has made me queasy. I don't want to spoil everyone's lunch." He got up and politely bowed to the group before Herr Farber could comment. He caught Katalyna's eyes. She was not happy. Too bad. Why in the world did she accept the invitation from those miserable people?

He made it to his seat and leaned back. A nap was in order. He put his hat over his face.

"Attention," the uniformed conductor said as he walked the length of the train car, "we will be arriving in Szczecin in twenty minutes. Please have your documents."

Pyotr froze. What if he was found out? What if they wouldn't allow him to get to Berlin? His family? Yakob? His mind and heart raced. His hands turned cold. He had trouble swallowing. He must gain his composure. He forced himself to breathe and focused on the passing scenery from the window. A Chopin melody came to him. He closed his eyes for a second or two and began to hum. It was all right. His papers were in order. His Polish looks had never betrayed him. No one knew except, no... Katalyna. How would she... She didn't. Not eating pork? It was too expensive. He could only afford the strudel. Reichsmarks only went so far. He sat up. Everyone appeared at ease. The border was not an issue for them.

The door that separated his car from the next opened and Katalyna stepped through. She came towards him.

"Herr Doktor, my seat," she pointed.

He stood to let her pass.

"You shouldn't have left," she said in a low voice. She took out a hairbrush from her purse.

"He was a boor."

She ran the brush with brisk strokes through her hair several times. "That's precisely why."

"I don't understand."

She stared at him and then picked up her purse to put the brush away. "Oh, you are too much," she laughed, "your innocence is...charming, to the point of either calculation or stupidity. Do you think Herr Farber and his *stummen kopf*, dumb head girlfriend, only happened to be on the train?"

"I don't... I didn't think..."

"Nothing happens by chance. When I got to the dining car, it was as if they were waiting."

He folded his hands in front of him. "What are you talking about? There is nothing to hide. This is a business trip. I'm not some thief or criminal. Maybe..." He turned to her and stared.

"Oh, Professor, apple strudel instead of pork schnitzel. What could be the reason?"

He hoped he didn't blush. "It's hard to admit, but it's finance. A professor's salary is not large."

"So it was money." She seemed to think about it. "I'm sorry to have thought anything else."

He knew he should end this discussion. She was given a plausible explanation. An *adwokat* friend once advised about the danger of asking one too many questions. In music, it was squeezing too many notes into a measure.

"Why did you think I didn't order the schnitzel?" Good advice is only good if heeded.

Katalyna stared into Pyotr's eyes and then looked away. "Don't say anything, Professor, but we both know. Your behavior betrays you. The others on this train could not care less about the Germans, but you do, from the moment you sat down."

He opened his mouth, but there were no words. He heard the whoosh of the train passing through the countryside.

"I know these things," she said.

He wanted to ask how, and act offended, but he wasn't skilled in duplicity, particularly when he lived a lie. "Think whatever you like, Pania Paternoskov," he said, his voice strained.

"I won't inform on you, Professor. It is our secret."

He rubbed his chin with his hand.

"You don't need to say thank you either," she said. "You're probably married and have children. I do it for them."

"How do you know such things about me? Are you with the *policja*? Spy?"

"Neither of them, but I'm right, yes, Professor?"

He had never encountered such a woman. Forceful, smart, independent, and, he had to admit, pretty. Her dark eyes complemented her angular face. It was not Slavic even though she had mentioned she worked for some cultural organization from Czechoslovakia. It was more French or perhaps Germanic. How could he be thinking such things when sitting next to him was a *dybbuk*, an evil spirit? He reached for a last shred of argument.

"Pania Paternoskov."

She gave him a frosty stare.

"I mean Katalyna. I am not what you think. My last name is spelled with an 'i' not a 'y,' *Rakowski*.

"Then you have misspelled your own name. Listen to me, when the Germans board this train, I am sure Herr Farber will point to us."

"Us?"

"To him we are a couple."

"My God."

"There are worse things, my Professor."

Her face was animated and became more beautiful as she revealed her plan.

"We are traveling to Berlin for a conference on music and culture. You are the guest speaker who will discuss great composers including Chopin, Liszt—"

"Mahler?"

"Mahler is Jewish. He is not part of your speech."

"I'll discuss Beethoven, instead."

She smiled. "There is hope for you yet."

## Chapter Fifteen

# 1975 - Chicago

United Flight 470 landed at O'Hare Airport in Chicago during dinnertime. Jack wasn't surprised there was no one to greet him. He was an only child and his mother... Well, his mother... He hadn't thought of her in a while—a long while. He followed the other arrivals down the lengthy corridor. Signs hung from the ceiling directing them to the "Main Terminal" and "Baggage." People rushed in the other direction to catch their flights. Their faces were filled with anticipation. On his side, the crowd moved along, resigned, so it seemed, to their destination and the resumption of their lives. He caught the sound of a ball game, and looked up. There was a bar in the main area of the terminal. Highlights of Boston's game played on the TV screen. What the hell? He'd stay for a drink, and watch. It was the height of rush hour. A cab ride would take at least an hour to get downtown to Northwestern Memorial Hospital. He found a spot at the bar.

"What'cha having?" the bartender asked.

"Johnny Black on the rocks." Jack watched him pour and then turned his attention to the TV. It was a good day for Boston. They whipped the Reds 6, zip. El Tiante was on top of his game. He took a sip of his drink, then looked around. There were two men sitting a seat away. They were dressed in suits, probably businessmen who were in a heavy discussion about putting more money on the rest of the series. Near them, almost at the corner, was a woman. She appeared to be by herself. She wore a white blouse. Her jacket was on an empty chair between her and one of the men. Jack figured her to be in her late twenties or early thirties. A glass of white wine was in front of her. He went back to the TV. He sensed movement and turned in the direction of the woman. She raised her glass. He paused and then did the same. The two businessmen discussed odds and percentages. Jack took another swig and put the drink down. He heard Luis Tiant being interviewed and looked up.

"I had real good stuff, Curt, the hitters couldn't catch up to my pitches," Tiant said. "I throw the fast ball and then a slow curve."

Jack smiled. That's what passed for a great interview. He was no better.

The bartender took his old glass and put a fresh drink in front of him. "Compliments of the lady," he said.

Jack turned.

"Mind if I join you?" she asked.

She sat down next to Jack. "I saw you watching the ball game. I love baseball and the World Series is…"

He smiled. "So do I."

"Who you rooting for?"

"Boston."

She took a sip of her wine and gave him a mischievous look. "Who's going to win?"

"Are you kidding? Boston."

"Of course, who isn't? I love what the Red Sox are doing. It's so much fun to watch.

"To the Red Sox," he said and held up his glass. She joined in the toast.

He put his drink down. She was even better looking up

close. She had shoulder-length dark hair that played off her tan. "Thanks for the cocktail. Flying gets me thirsty."

"You're right about that. I just got in from California. The crowd was too much. I thought I'd wait it out and have a drink before braving a cab. Are you coming or going?"

"Both."

She smiled. "At the same time?"

He shook his head. "No, just staying long enough to see someone. Then I have to leave."

She gave him an inquiring look, but didn't ask. "Chicago is a great town. My business takes me here often."

"Yeah? What do you do?"

"I'm a rep for Gallo."

"Wine?"

"Yep," and pointed to her glass.

Jack stretched out in his seat and ordered another round. He was starting to feel good. He loosened his tie and unbuttoned the top button of his shirt.

"Gallo, huh. Is that like Boone's Farm or Ripple?"

"Very funny." She ran her finger up the side of the glass. "Well, some of it is. We have the cheap wine in a jug and then there's some real high quality."

"If I were to guess," he said, pointing his finger at her, "high quality is your thing."

She drew in a breath. "Why, thank you…"

"Jack. Jack Rakow."

She stuck out her hand. "Linzie Stevens. Wait a minute, I've heard of you. Jack Rakow. Where did I hear that name?"

He laughed. "About five minutes ago."

"Huh?"

"On the TV. The sports announcer."

Her eyes widened. "Holy shit, you're the pitcher who had an emergency and flew to Chicago for a relative."

"That's me."

The two businessmen stopped their discussions. The bald-headed one turned in his seat while his partner's mouth dropped.

Jack gave them a half-hearted wave. "You want to go?" He motioned to the bartender for the bill. "We can share a cab if you're going into the city." He looked past Linzie to see if the men were coming toward him.

"Sure. I'm staying at the Ambassador West."

"Wow, Gallo treats you well."

"They're our customer. In sales, one hand washes the other."

He looked at her and hoped that axiom would continue to apply.

*Chapter Sixteen*

# Warsaw, Poland - 1937

The train approached the station at Szczecin. At least a dozen Nazi flags hung from the rafters several feet apart. Pyotr could see groups of soldiers lined up on the platform. The screech of metal on metal temporarily blocked out all other sound as the train slowed, then slid to a stop. As if a play was to begin, quiet crept through his car...not of anticipation, but of fear.

A shrill whistle sounded and was repeated along the length of the train. Seconds later the car doors opened and the soldiers boarded. There were distant shouts coming from other parts of the train. The yelling became more distinct as the sounds came closer. The door that connected Pyotr's car to the other was flung open.

"*Haben ihr dokumente.* Have your documents out," shouted a soldier who looked like someone's little brother. Behind him were three uniformed men. Those behind the young man snatched up each document and examined it. They compared the photographs to the person. Seconds ticked by and then one of the soldiers said, "*Ja,*" and the passenger sat back and put his papers back into his pocket.

Pyotr glanced at Katalyna. She touched his hand. "It will be all right," she said. "I've been through this many times.

Their purpose is to make you uncomfortable, but then they'll leave you alone."

The group of men came closer and stopped several rows in front of them. An older man with a trim beard handed them his papers.

"*Sie gehen mit ihm. Ihre Papiere sind nicht in ordnung . Sind Sie ein Jude?* You go with him. Your papers are not in order. Are you a Jew?"

"*Nein, Ich bin kein Jude.* No I am not a Jew," the older man said. His voice cracked. "Please, I am from Prague. My wife is waiting in Berlin. I am not a Jew."

He was grabbed, then pushed out the door. Pyotr looked out the window and saw the man lose his balance and fall to the ground.

"*Steh auf!* Get up." A soldier seized the man's arm and dragged him toward the station.

"My God," Pyotr said under his breath. "Animals."

"Good evening, Herr Professor."

Pyotr spun his gaze from the window. To his shock, Herr Farber and his blonde girlfriend stood in front of him. The civilian clothes were gone. Instead each had a brown shirt with a swastika armband. Out of the corner of his eye, he glimpsed the color drain from Katalyna's face. He cleared his throat. "Herr Farber, how nice to see you and Frau Bauer, again. I did not …"

"Oh, Professor, of course you did not know. That is what Frau Bauer and I do. You are not the first or the last. Please stand up."

"Herr Farber…" he said as he rose, clutching his documents.

Farber motioned for him to step back. "Frau Paternoskov, your papers."

She handed her passport and travel forms. She didn't look at Pyotr.

Farber took out a pair of pince-nez glasses and studied

them. He held up her passport. "Ah, Frau Paternoskov, under religion, it is blank. A mistake?"

"No, I told the clerk I was an agnostic."

"What kind of religion is that?" Farber asked.

"The clerk gave me a choice, atheist or agnostic. I hedged my bet."

Farber put his glasses back in his pocket. He half turned to Frau Bauer, who grinned. "You must be a free thinker, Frau Paternoskov. Aren't you?"

"I do not understand your question."

"Jews are free thinkers. They make things up to confuse others. Is that what you do?"

"Herr Farber, I am a representative of the Gesellschaft für Musik und Literatur für Czechoslovakia, the Society of Music and Literature for Czechoslovakia. I travel throughout Europe to organize lectures on books, music, and yes, sometimes ideas. In Berlin—"

"It is what I thought. I admit that Frau Bauer and I were a little fooled at lunch. You travel with a man who is obviously Polish. You ordered pork and ate your schnitzel with relish." He wagged his index finger. "But then we thought smart Jews would do that too. They are clever people. Yes? Of course they're clever, they run everything, but no longer." He nodded to two soldiers. "*Nehmen diese Jude Hündin aus . Ich werde ihr später zu besuchen.* Take this Jew bitch out. I will attend to her later."

The soldiers pushed Pyotr out of the way and grabbed his seatmate. For an instant he saw her face. Her eyes were defiant. She did not scream or cry.

"Take your hands off of me," she said. Her voice was low but authoritative. The soldiers froze and looked at Farber. She stood and edged herself into the aisle.

"If you are taking me off the train, Herr Farber, I will go without any assistance. But you are making a grave mistake."

They stared at each other and then Farber raised his right hand and slapped her hard across the face.

"No Jude Hündin talks to me that way. We are on German soil. You will do as I say. Out."

# Chapter Seventeen

# 1975 - Chicago

Jack stood in the cab line at the airport and within seconds a taxi appeared.

"Whaddyah know. That was quick," he said. He and Linzie settled in and the cab took off. Traffic seemed to have disappeared.

"This is better than I thought," she said.

He leaned towards her. "Stopping for a drink can lead to good things."

She smiled and moved closer to him.

He put his arm around her and kissed her lips. She didn't hold back. This was going to be one hell of a ride.

The trip was one long passionate kiss. The driver had to repeat himself a couple of times to get their attention.

"Ma'am, we be at your hotel. We're at the Ambassador West."

Jack realized the car wasn't moving and someone was talking. He opened his eyes and recognized where they were. "Linzie, we're at your hotel."

She sat up and looked around. "Holy crap." She dug into her purse for her brush and mirror. After a few strokes, she rebuttoned three of the buttons on her blouse and applied a little lipstick. "There, how do I look?"

"Like you just got off an airplane, all prim and proper," he said.

"Hmm, let me think about that, the prim and proper part. Things were getting interesting."

He touched the back of her neck.

"Why don't I check in and then I'll meet you at the bar," she said.

"Great idea."

They stepped out of the cab. Their luggage was already on the sidewalk. The driver stood by and waited. Jack grabbed his wallet.

"No, this is on the company," she said.

"I can get used to that." He took a step toward his bag but then turned toward her. "You know I'd love to continue what we started, but I've got to see my dad. He's at Northwestern. That's why I'm here. The telegram said urgent."

"Oh, of course. That's important." She looked at her watch. "It's probably after visiting hours. You should call the hospital."

He checked the time. 7:00 o'clock. "You may be right. I'll find a pay phone while you register."

"Jack, this is the Ambassador West. The pay phones are across from check-in."

He probably had a dumb look on his face. He picked up his bag and followed her into the hotel.

She kissed him on the cheek and then pointed out the phones.

"It won't take long," she said. "The hotel knows me."

He kept his eyes fixed on her. His imagination made up for what he couldn't see. A few seconds passed until he shook himself from his reverie and moved toward the phones. The telegram had the hospital's number and he dialed.

"Northwestern Memorial Hospital, how may I help you?" asked the operator.

"Ah, my dad is a patient and I'd like to see him."

"What is his name?"

"Peter Rakow. He's in intensive care."

"Just a minute. Yes, Mr. Rakow is here."

"Can you connect me?"

"Patients in the ICU do not have phones. I'll transfer your call to the nurses station."

"Okay, thanks."

"One minute."

Jack listened to the click of the lines. He turned and peeked at Linzie who stood next to the counter. She appeared to be in a conversation with a well-dressed man. He caught Linzie's seductive laugh while he held the phone an inch or two away. He heard two clicks and put the phone back to his ear. "Hello?" The call went dead. He looked at the phone swore and put another quarter into the slot. Another operator answered but this time the call transfer reached a nurse. He was about to speak when he felt a hand on his back. He looked over and saw Linzie behind him.

A small smile crossed her face. She dangled a key on her finger. "1007," she whispered.

"Just a minute," he spoke into the phone and then covered the mouthpiece. "1007, got it. I'll be up there…" He rolled his eyes.

"Don't be too long. I have wine that's chilling and Jack, it's the good stuff." She gave him a pat on his ass and left.

## Chapter Eighteen

# 2015 – Chicago

Billy Dee played with his empty beer can, digesting what the sports reporter Melissa told him. "He didn't come back, huh? You mean for the World Series or ever."

"He was gone for about three years. He hung it up in 1980 or '81." She eyed her empty glass. "It was '81. Believe it or not, he was on the Dodgers. They beat the Yankees in six games."

"You sure?"

"It's what I do but you can Google it."

He raised his eyes. "Nah, I use a flip phone. Don't need all that other stuff."

"Really? I couldn't live without my smartphone." She pulled her iPhone out of her bag. She pressed a few buttons and the screen lit up. "See, Rakow is on the Dodger 1981 roster."

Billy Dee grabbed his glasses from his pocket. "So the lucky son of a bitch was on three teams that went to the World Series. Ernie Banks played almost twenty years and never saw the glory."

"Baseball can be cruel."

"Nah, it's life's challenge. You have to make lemonade out of the lemons you sometimes get, and old Ernie did. So Ms. Sports Reporter, where did Rakow go for those three years he didn't play?"

"Great question. You ever see the movie *The Natural*?"

He rubbed his face. "Sounds familiar. That was the movie where old baseball players came out of a corn field, and the guy, hold on, Kevin Costner, built a stadium in the middle of nowhere."

She shook her head. "Wrong baseball movie. That was *Field of Dreams*."

He looked at her. "Okay, let me think. *The Natural*. I know I saw it. My wife is good at this, she'd know." He rolled the beer can several times between his hands. "It's coming to me. It was based on a book. The guy who wrote it had a funny name. Melman or something like that."

"You're close."

He slapped the table. "Paul Newman was in it, and he conned this gangster dude out of his money." He smiled from ear to ear.

"Sorry, that was *The Sting*. In *The Natural*, Robert Redford played this talented baseball player who met a woman. She was crazy and shot him. It took him ten years to get back to the majors."

"You think Jack Rakow got shot?"

"I'm guessing whatever happened then may have something to do with the present."

He stopped smiling and held the beer can in his hand. "You've been playing me. Jesus. I knew better than to have this drink. Damn." He slapped the table with his hands. "Who's been leaking? Who's been telling you all the shit about me and what's gone down at the station?"

"I haven't played you, Officer Jackson. Why in the world would I do that? I'm trying to give you context. I don't know how Jack Rakow disappeared, but knowing some of his history may help."

Billy Dee gave her a stern look, but after a few seconds softened. "True, but let's get the first thing out of the way."

*Chapter Nineteen*

# Berlin - 1937

The train was about to pull out of the station at Szczecin. Katalyna's seat was empty, like a half dozen others. He had watched the soldiers shove her out the door. Unlike the older man who fell, she kept her balance as well as composure. Pyotr looked out the window and followed their movement. He heard orders barked, and the doors clanged shut. He stared at the outside scene. *What will become of her? Where will those animals take her?* He was so lost in thought that he jumped when he felt a tap on his shoulder. Herr Farber leaned over the empty seat, his face inches from him.

"Forgive me, Herr Docktor, for startling you. Words of advice. If your desire is for a Jew whore, have more discretion. I happen to like you, so you do not have to worry, but next time you may not be so lucky. Enjoy Berlin, it's a beautiful city. Heil Hitler." He gave Pyotr's shoulder a pat and marched off the train.

Pyotr glared at Faber's receding back. If his eyes had been weapons, that little man would have been annihilated. A minute or two passed, and he lurched in his seat as the train began to accelerate. The soldiers standing in groups at the station soon became specks. "Good-bye, Katalyna," he said softly, "I pray for you." He took out a handkerchief and wiped his eyes.

A conductor entered the car. He wasn't the same one who'd announced their arrival into Germany. Even the uniform was different. He took out a heavy gold watch from his waistcoat. In a clipped German accent, he informed the passengers in German, French, and English they would arrive in Berlin in about two hours. Polish and other Slavic languages didn't rate. The conductor left. The passengers' silence of a few minutes ago was replaced by escalating whispers and then full-blown conversations. The people in front of Pyotr spoke in a tone loud enough for him to hear. They thanked their God and then suggested Katalyna was not just a Jew but also a spy. He caught a few glances in his direction. When he looked, they averted their eyes.

He sat back in his seat. He should also be thanking his God, his Jewish God, but he couldn't bring himself to do it. He was spared this time, but for how much longer? The future had become the present, and it was getting darker by the minute. Europe was finished. Poland was only a step or two behind Germany in its policies toward the Jews. He and his family had to get out and leave this madness. There was no safe place, maybe France or England, but neither had a history of welcoming Jewish refugees. He could feel his heart pound. He stomped on the floor of the car. He visualized shaking his fist at God and in exasperation said to himself, "*Got im himmel*, God in heaven, what have You done?" His foot struck something underneath his seat. Without being obvious, he moved the object to where he could reach down and grab it in one quick motion. It was an envelope. He put his hat on his lap and placed the packet inside. The writing was in French. He silently thanked Chopin for his life in France. "*Livrer immédiatement*. Deliver immediately." A note that must have been written in Katalyna's handwriting was on the side of the envelope. "Pyotr, *Je te mets en grave danger mais la liberté en Tchecoslavaquie en depend. Que Dieu soit avec toi cela d'un non-croyant.* I am placing you in great danger but freedom depends on it, Czechoslovakia depends on it. May God be with you—this from a nonbeliever."

## Chapter Twenty

# 1975 - Chicago

Jack listened to the nurse on the other end of the phone.

"Your father...stroke...heart," the nurse said.

"Uh-huh. Is it serious?" Jack asked.

"Well, sir, did you say you're his son?"

"Yeah, my dad's only."

"It's as serious as it can get. ...coma."

"Coma? My dad? What?" He had to admit his mind had been elsewhere. The nurse now sounded exasperated.

"Your father suffered a stroke. Are you listening? His heart is also failing."

"Holy shit," he said more to himself. "I-I didn't know. Can I see him?"

"Not tonight. I think it would be best to come tomorrow morning."

"Are you sure? I'm a few blocks away."

She paused. "I'm sorry. Visiting hours are over and this unit is very strict."

"How early?"

"7:00 a.m."

"Okay." He hung up the phone, but didn't move for a few seconds. The news settled over him. He walked from the phone booth to the elevator. Did Linzie say 1007 or 1003? Shit. What was he doing? His father was dying...

the hell with getting laid. He stepped back and looked for a place to sit. To have heard a human voice tell him his dad was near death was different than reading a telegram. The seriousness of the situation exploded. He looked up from his seat near the check-in area. There was a crowd of people—all seemingly happy going about their business.

"Jesus." This wasn't a baseball game where, win or lose, there was a tomorrow. His father will be gone…forever. No appeals. "Huh." He gazed down at the carpeted floor. He focused on the intricate pattern of the design and the interlocking of the colors. He found no relief. He stood.

His father, for most of Jack's life, had emphasized the positive. Despite what his dad had been through in the war, he was an optimist. A believer that life was worth living.

Jack walked toward the big windows that surrounded the large open space he was in. He saw the tree-lined street with expensive graystone buildings and beautiful people rushing to the fabulous places nearby.

His father had come to Chicago with nothing but a ten-dollar gift from H.I.A.S., a Jewish organization that aided immigrants. Dad was not a bitter man, despite having lost everything. He refused to live in the past. He adapted, even shortened the family name. Jack thought back to the arguments he'd had with him about college. In the end, his father supported him when he left school to play baseball.

As a kid, Jack had a sense his parents were different from the other families on the block. He intuitively knew that underneath his father's perpetual smile lurked a sadness. The melancholy would come out of nowhere—at a park, singing the Star-Spangled Banner, eating a good dinner. It would flash across his father's face and then the feeling of heaviness was gone.

When Jack was ten or eleven, his mother left. That was one of the few times he saw his father cry. His grief didn't last long. About a week later, his dad pulled him aside. Jack hadn't picked up his glove or watched a ball game during that week. His dad put his arm around him and said, "I vant you to know. Your mother is a good person. Ve tried. It didn't work. The var never left her. I can't live that way. That vas a long time ago. I don't forget, but I can't let it rule me."

That was it. We went on.

***

Jack heard the bell of the elevator. He turned from the window. Laughter came from the bar area. He saw couples holding hands. People with luggage walked in from the outside. What the hell? He couldn't visit him. How he spent this night won't change anything. His dad would understand. He was practical. "Yankaleh," he'd say, "alvays seize an opportunity. Those tings don't vait."

Jack smiled at how real his dad's voice sounded.

He went toward the elevator and waited. The door opened and he got in. He pushed the button. It was for the 10th floor.

*Chapter Twenty-One*

# Berlin – 1937

Pyotr gazed at the passengers. The envelope, under his hat, was resting on his lap. More trouble. What had happened to his life? Days ago, or was it just a day, he was a professor of music doing what he loved…teaching. How did he become an informant, a courier, a spy? Oh, his God must be laughing at his predicament. What was that saying? *Menschen plan und Gott Lacht.* Man plans and God laughs. His sides must be hurting for this joke He has played. Pyotr's fingers ran up and down the sides of his hat. Who needs more danger? He bent forward as if to pick something from the floor, instead he placed the envelope inside his jacket. He could go to the lavatory and flush the letter. That would end one problem. He didn't have to reread her note to be reminded of its importance. Freedom in Czechoslovakia depends on… Oh, Katalyna, why him? Why the devil did he pick this seat? He looked out the window. Cows grazed undisturbed by the rushing train. An occasional tractor belched smoke as it went between rows of crops. He turned from the window and stared at the back of the seat ahead of him. What were they doing to Katalyna? She'd certainly been mistreated, but would Faber and his whorish friend Bauer use torture on a woman? Had Germany stepped back centuries to when the

Huns butchered their way through Europe? He smacked his forehead with his fist. It was too much.

He looked between the seats and saw his crinkled newspaper, *Der Stürmer*. He didn't grab it. He stared at it and realized the horror of that garbage. As the public drank in those lies, it made it easier for Faber and his crowd to do what they wanted. He gave the outside of his breast pocket a pat. He had become a soldier in the still unannounced war on civilization. He hadn't realized until this moment he had enlisted.

\*\*\*

The train pulled into the Lehrter Bahnhof in Berlin. The station, much like the one in Warsaw, was massive. People scurried from one platform to the other. A train pulled in and another one left. A conductor blew his whistle and an engine roared. With his valise in hand, Pyotr walked with the crowd from his train. The line was orderly as he stepped through the doors to the outside. There was no rain and he had to squint into the setting sun. In every direction, Nazi flags flew from each building.

He decided to walk instead of taking a cab. The Polish foreign office was kind enough to provide him with a tourist map. He studied it. He was in the *Mitte* section. The envelope that Katalyna gave him was addressed to a Frederick Kaddoch, Adlon Hotel, across from the Brandenburg Gate. He located it on his map along with the British and American embassies that were nearby. The Jewish area called *Scheunenviertel* (Barn Quarter) was also within walking distance of that hotel.

Cars and people were everywhere. Unlike Warsaw, if there were beggars, they were not seen. No garbage or papers littered the sidewalks. Stores even at this hour were full of shoppers. Every few blocks men, dressed in brown shirts, black pants, high leather boots, and Nazi armbands stood on the corners. They, like the flags that flew in the breeze, reminded everyone of the Nazi presence.

He gawked at the sights around him. It was only nineteen years since Germany had lost the Great War, but there were no signs of defeat. There was a vibrancy not felt in Warsaw. He stopped at a bakery. The store still had a small line of customers. He ordered an apple strudel and a koffee and took a seat near the window. He took a bite. The strudel melted in his mouth. At least in one respect Herr Farber was right: German apple strudel was delicious. He put another piece on his fork and was about to enjoy another bite.

"*Entschuldigen Sie mich, aber ich muss für Unterlagen fragen.* Excuse me, but I must ask to see your papers."

He put his arm down and rested the fork on the plate. He stared at her. She was young, dressed in a yellow apron with her thick blonde hair tied in a bun. "You want to see my papers? May I ask why?"

Her eyes rolled toward the ceiling as if he'd asked a stupid question.

"I am not from here. I'm on a business trip."

"It is obvious you are not from here. There is a law in Germany that no business can serve Jews. Are you a Jew?"

He hesitated for a second. "Of course not. I am Polish." He went into his coat pocket. "Here." Katalyna's envelope along with his passport book was in his hand. He motioned for her to take the passport.

"What is the packet?" she asked.

"A letter I forgot to mail." His calmness surprised him. Inside, fear ripped through him. She took his document and he returned the letter to his coat pocket.

She glanced through the pages, then handed the passport

back. "Sorry to have inconvenienced you, but one cannot be too careful."

"I understand." He picked up his fork. His hand was steady.

"I am going to the post soon and will be happy to mail your letter."

He held the fork halfway from the plate to his mouth. "Don't trouble yourself…"

"No, mein herr, it is not a bother. It is rude to ask for identification. I don't like it, but I have to. It's the least I can do."

## Chapter Twenty-Two

# 2015 - Chicago

"All right, Officer Jackson, you've been fair with me. I'll tell you what I know," Melissa said. She focused her attention on the bartender while she spoke.

"You can't wave old Pat down. He don't see nothin' unless you're in front of him."

"Are you serious?"

Billy Dee smiled. "If you had a C note in your hand, he may notice. Otherwise…"

"Gotcha. I'll get another round."

"Not for me."

"Come on, you're not on duty."

"That's okay. I got to report to the captain who must be thinkin'—I don't know what."

She leaned on her elbows. Her eyes sparkled.

"You can't let a lady drink alone."

He checked his watch. He should have been at the station a half hour ago. Shit. "I'm calling in to let them know something had come up."

"Make it sound good, Officer Jackson," as she made her way to the bar.

He arched his eyebrows and dialed his sergeant. He had to move the phone from his ear as Flynn's voice blasted

83

through the receiver. "Where the hell are you?" The Captain has gone ballistic. His phone is ringing off the hook. Somehow the press has gotten wind of it."

"Shit." Billy Dee spoke softly into the phone while he kept an eye on Melissa. "Listen, Sarge, you're going to have to make do for a little longer—"

"What the hell you talking about, Billy Dee? I just told you, the captain—"

"Yeah, I know, but look…" He watched Melissa start her walk back to the table. "I got to make this quick. There's a leak in the police station. I'm trying to find out—" He hit the disconnect button.

She brought the drinks to the table. "You look like you swallowed a canary. Everything cool with the boss?"

"If a squadron don't show up here looking for me, everything is fine."

"In that case, here's to their health." She raised her glass and waited for him.

"You goin' to get me drunk. Ah, what the hell." He picked up his beer can and toasted her glass. "I never tire of a good beer." He looked at the can. "Where the hell did Pat find this Pabst?"

"It's my charm, Officer. Can I call you Billy Dee?"

He gave it a few seconds thought. "Why not?"

Her face glowed; whether it was from the booze or natural, he didn't know or care. If nothing else, this was fun, and that was something that hadn't come his way in a long while. He took another swig. The liquid got his taste buds jangling. He was hungry. "You don't know it, but Pat can make a mean burger with all the fixings. Interested?"

She made a face. "I'm more vegetarian. Don't get me wrong, I don't look down on meat eaters but…"

"No meat? Girl, you'll smoke a cigar, but you have a problem with beef?"

"Not a problem. I just avoid it whenever possible."

He shook his head and reached for his Pabst. He brought it to his mouth but didn't drink. He put the can down. "Okay, Melissa, tell me what you know."

"That was abrupt. From a burger to information. You change speeds at a fast pace, Billy Dee." She took a sip of her drink and then licked her lips. "How about a salad? I guess I'm hungry too."

"How about you telling me something so when I get back to the station I don't get fired."

She put her drink down and hauled her purse onto the table. She rummaged through it. "Where the hell is the damn thing? Aha, got it." She took out a slender rectangular gadget. "You know what this is?"

He leaned toward her. "Come on, Melissa, I'm not ancient. That's a scanner."

She seemed disappointed. "Oh. Shit. I guess that won't work."

He drummed his fingers. "Melissa, this isn't a game. Rakow could be in danger or he escaped. Either way, we have to find him."

"Okay, okay, I can't name names, but I, Jesus I can't believe I'm going to do this…"

"If it makes it easier, tell me where to look."

She stared straight at him. "Civilians."

"Civilians?" Billy Dee asked. "What civilians?"

Melissa set her purse on the floor. "Come on, Billy Dee, do I have to spoon-feed you? Aren't there regular people working at the station."

"Of course. Civvys do all sorts of… Oh shit. The fingerprint…" His voice drifted off. "We got to go. Now."

"Okay, could you drop me off closer to Lake Shore Drive?"

"What?"

"It's easier to get a cab from there."

"Melissa, I'm not your damn chauffeur. I don't have time for that."

"You can't leave me here. This isn't a great spot to flag down a taxi."

"I'll have Pat call for one."

"*Please*. At this hour of the night it will take you five minutes."

He got up and strode to the door. "We're good, Pat?"

The bartender nodded. "Your friend is welcome anytime. Much better to look at than your ugly mug."

"You can have her." He stepped outside and without waiting walked toward the parking lot. A car raced by travelling in the opposite direction. Didn't even slow down at the intersection. Jesus, what was that guy's hurry? He stopped a few feet from his Chrysler 200. There was not another vehicle on the road. Shit. He turned toward the bar. "Melissa, come on, I'll—"

She walked towards him. He could see she had a smile. "You're a gentleman, Billy Dee."

He was about twenty-five feet from her.

The roar of an engine grabbed his attention. A car with its headlights off sped toward them. He heard the screech of tires. Someone leaned out of the passenger window. *Pop, pop, pop*. Melissa screamed and staggered to the ground. Before Billy Dee could draw his weapon, the car sped off.

"Oh my God." He rushed towards her. "Melissa, Melissa." She lay on the sidewalk. He placed his hand on her neck and felt for a pulse. Thank God, she still had one.

Pat came running from the bar. "What happened?"

"She's shot, I think she caught it in the legs. Call an ambulance, 911. Hurry."

Pat sprinted back inside.

"Say something, girl," Billy Dee said as he held her.

"God, I hurt. Menstrual cramps has nothing on this."

"Hang in there, you'll be all right. An ambulance is on its way." He took off his jacket and placed it under her head. Sirens screamed in the distance.

Pat charged toward them. "They're on their way."

## Chapter Twenty-Three

# 1975 - Chicago

There was a small doorbell adjacent to the entrance of 1007. Jack smiled. *It's the Ambassador West.* He rang the bell and waited. He pushed the button again and then tried the door. It opened. The light from the outside hallway streamed into the darkened foyer.

"Linzie? Hello."

"I'm in the bedroom. Follow the sound of my voice."

The suite was dark. "Mind if I turn on a light?"

"Go ahead. The switch is on the wall to your left."

He flicked it on. Soft light lit the room. He let the entrance door close.

"Cozy place you have." He draped his jacket over a chair in the living room.

"They do treat us well."

He left his shoes and a small travel bag on the thick white carpet next to the same chair, then crossed the room. The bedroom door was partially closed. "Should I knock or just come in?"

"Well, what would a gentleman do?"

He sighed and knocked. "May I come in?"

"Of course, silly."

He pushed the door farther. The room was huge. There were floor to ceiling windows that looked out at the darkening city. A canopied king-size bed was in the middle with Linzie propped on pillows. She had wrapped herself in an off- white linen sheet. A glass of wine was in her hand.

"Welcome to Chicago, Jack. Take a hot shower and relax. The bathroom is over to the right. Drinks and further delights will be waiting."

"Can't refuse that. How about a drink before I go?"

"There's a fully stocked bar in the powder room."

"The what?"

"Washroom."

The sheet that covered her dropped slightly and revealed the top of a lacey black negligee.

"I won't be long."

She smiled. "I wouldn't think so."

He gave her a kiss on the way. The bathroom was big enough to hold a small party. A bar was beneath one of the vanities. He helped himself to a glass of Johnny Black. While he sipped, he turned on the shower and waited a few seconds. Water streamed not only from the ceiling of the glass-encased stall but the sides. "Holy shit. It doesn't get much better." He slipped off his clothes and stepped in. *Baseball locker rooms should have something like this.* This setup would extend his pitching career.

A panel of buttons adjusted the spray and temperature. He could spend a lot of time playing with all the adjustments, something to look forward to later. He finished with his shower and stepped out. A plush genderless bathrobe hung near the towels. He put it on. An array of cologne selections rested on a silver-like platter near one of the sinks. He slapped some on, brushed his hair and teeth. He caught his image in one of the mirrors. He was ready.

"Look at you. Did you enjoy yourself in there?"

"Are you kidding? That bathroom was something else."

She pulled back the covers and he saw her bare leg and

thigh. "Champagne?" She put her wine down on the night-stand and reached for the bottle and a new glass.

He sat on the bed wanting to grab her body. She was the definition of hot. He watched her slide over to him. Be cool, he thought. "Champagne? Gallo makes that stuff?" Jesus, she had long legs and one gorgeous ass partially hidden by her bikini underwear.

"Here," she said.

He took the glass and poured.

"Let's drink to Boston winning the Series," she said.

"Yeah, to Boston." He clinked her glass. Her eyes were bright. She took a sip.

"Hey, slugger, come closer." She wrapped her arms around him and let her glass fall on the carpeted floor. "Let's play ball."

***

"Goddamn that was…"

"Unbelievable," she said. "You baseball players have stamina."

"There were others?"

"Of course not, well, not ball players. Hey, don't give me that look. I know I'm not your first."

He smiled. "No, no, but…"

"You're a guy, so it's all right? Please. Travelling is boring as hell. You know that. We had fun. It breaks the monotony." She rolled off him. "I have to go to the bathroom. Don't move. I'll be right back."

He watched her. *What a piece,* he told himself. God, that was great. He fluffed several pillows and sat up. He heard a sound.

"Is that you, Linzie?"

The closet door opened. A man dressed in a dark suit

stepped out. "Nah, it ain't Linzie. You and her look good on film." A camera hung from his neck and he had a gun in his hand.

"What the hell? Who the fuck and what are you—" Jack put one foot on the floor.

"I'd get your ass back in that bed and don't move." The man pointed his gun.

Jack sat back. "Okay, what is this about?" His breath came rapidly.

The man chuckled. "What is this about? Why, it's about you and Linzie. You two are the stars…well, actually, you're the star. Linzie, get out here and properly introduce yourself."

The bathroom door opened and she came out fully dressed. She moved a foot or two behind the man.

"Tell him, sweetheart," the man said.

"It's a setup, Jack. I'm married. This is my husband, Gino Castellini. He works for an organization."

"Let me guess," Jack said.

"That's enough. I'll lay it out real simple. You're pitching the first game in Cincinnati. About the fourth inning, you lose your stuff. Nothing dramatic, but the curve ball flattens and your fastball ain't so fast. Capeesh?"

Jack looked from the man to Linzie and back again. "And if I don't?"

The man's face broke into a huge grin. "This will make a nice story. Pitcher goes to visit dad on his deathbed, winds up at the Ambassador West with a married woman…very bad publicity. You'll be on the front page of every newspaper in America. When the press gets through with you, you'll be dirt…less than dirt. In case you don't care about your reputation or career as an added incentive, who knows what could happen to my dear wife or your poor father. Mistakes are made every day."

"You fuckin'—"

"Hey, there's a lady present. Where's your manners?"

Jack gripped the sheet around his fist. He stared at Castellini. It occurred to him he had seen him before. Where was it? Shit.

"Have a good night and enjoy that bathroom again." He pushed his wife toward the door. "We'll be watching on Monday."

***

Jack didn't move from the bed. His brain shouted instructions—double lock the door. Call the police. Get the hell out of the room. Seconds ticked by. He strained to listen for sounds, any sounds. The room, though heated, turned cold, ice-like. He shivered and then his body shook. He grabbed the covers and drew them up over himself, but he couldn't stop. Sweat poured from him, but his teeth chattered. He put his head under the sheets and through force of will took deep breaths. He didn't know how long it took before he regained his composure. He lowered the blanket from his eyes and peeked. Nothing had changed. The room and everything in it was the same. He sat up. The Champagne bottle was still on the nightstand. He didn't bother with a glass. He took a large gulp and it caught in his throat. He spit it up. Shit. He jumped from the bed, bolted the front door using every lock, then trudged to the bathroom. He didn't care about the control panel for the shower. He washed up and found a bathrobe. He had to think. He moved toward the phone and lifted the receiver. He punched 9 and the line tone buzzed. He hit that digit again then 1, and stopped. What would he say? Was Castellini a real name? Was her name Linzie? If he did call, could they be listening? What if the threat to his father was genuine? He hung up. He rubbed his face with his hands. What to do?

In the past he would have called his dad… But now? This must be what his father felt during the war years…alone and afraid of unknown shadows.

Jesus, he should have asked his father more questions. He should have done a lot of things different. He lost Rookie of the Year and the chance to pitch for the Twins in the World Series because he acted with his dick. Now two lives were in danger as well as a game and his career.

He got up from the bed and moved to a high-back chair. *Think!* Instead, he stared into nothingness. His thoughts turned back to his father and his childhood.

He recalled the times after a meal or before he went to bed, he'd asked his father about the war. "What happened? How did you survive?"

Dad would hold him, but then look at the ceiling. With a sigh, he'd answer, "Luck." Jack could hear his father's voice. "Vhen you tink of all the close calls, it vas a miracle. I had a lot of *mazel*. I vas able to disappear a hundred times, before I vas caught."

"What were the close calls?" Jack had asked.

"Ach, too many to count. Life hung in the balance…every day. A stranger or a friend could either help or turn you in."

His father would then cover him and make sure he was all right. As he neared Jack's bedroom door, he turned, "You should never have to go through it."

\*\*\*

Jack stared at the vacant bed. Well, his father cannot help him now. He got dressed. It was four in the morning, a good hour after Linzie and her so-called husband had left. He went to the front entrance and unlocked it as quietly as he could. He twisted the knob and pulled the door open a crack. A shaft of light from the hallway streamed in. He opened it wider and looked in either direction. The corridor was deserted. He pulled the door shut and with his overnight bag walked to the elevator. The bell announcing its arrival sounded like an alarm. He glanced all around but nothing stirred. He got into the car and rode it to the ground level, bypassing reception.

"Would you like a cab, sir?" the doorman asked.

He was about to say yes, but caught himself. It was a new ball game. He was now in his father's world.

"That's okay," he told the man, "just out for a walk."

The attendant arched his eyebrows.

"Long night," he said, "need some air."

"I hear you, man. Have a nice one."

## Chapter Twenty-Four

# Berlin - 1937

"*Bitte, frau*," Pyotr said to the waitress in his best Berlin accent. "I am entrusted to deliver the letter. I had thought of the mail but even in Germany the post is not necessarily reliable. Thank you for your kindness."

The woman bowed her head slightly. "You speak German well, but you are not German."

"As I said, I am Polish, but German is required at the University where I teach."

He thought she was going to sit down and continue this unwanted conversation. Thank God, someone from the front of the bakery called her name.

"Gretta, there are more customers. Please."

She scowled. "Sorry, I must go."

He watched her walk away. He had lost his appetite but knew he couldn't leave. He put his hands under the table and rubbed them to revive circulation. How was he going to survive three more minutes, much less three days? He picked up his fork. His hand shook as he tried to pierce his pastry. He gazed around the room. Did anyone see? He put the fork down. He wouldn't dare try the coffee. He took several deep breaths. When he heard footsteps, he stopped. It was Gretta armed with a coffee pot coming toward him.

"Your cup has gone cold. I will get you a new one."

He wanted to refuse, but that could invite more conversation. "*Danke,*" he said and picked up the fork. "The strudel is wonderful."

"We are famous for it. We make the best in Berlin. Maybe all of Germany."

He smiled. "Well, then I'm most fortunate to start at the highest level."

She reached over and took a cup and saucer from another table. She placed them on his and poured. "Our koffee is also well known."

He hesitated and then reached for it. The liquid spilled onto the dish. "Ach, my hand. It acts up sometimes. The doctors don't know why."

"Or maybe it is nerves?"

He stared at her, then let out a laugh. "Nerves. That's a good one. I'll inform my doctor when I get home."

She put the coffee pot down and stood over him. "Is that letter something secret? It was in French."

God in heaven, all he wanted was something to eat. "*Bitte.*" He patted his coat pocket. "It's just a letter. That's all."

"May I see it again?"

He focused on the coffee cup in front of him. Who the hell was this girl? He was about to respond.

"Gretta, leave him be. He is a customer, a guest." The voice was the same as the one who had called her to the front.

He saw an older man in an apron walk towards them. The girl and the man conversed in rapid German. At the end, she stomped her foot and moved toward the front.

"You must excuse my daughter," the man said, "she is a member of Hitler Youth and wants to do her part for the Third Reich."

He grabbed his hat and valise. "She is enthusiastic."

The father grunted. "Yes," then lowered his voice, "everyone must be careful even with one's own children."

They looked at each other for a moment. Pyotr reached into his pocket and left a *rentenmark* on the table.

"It is too much for only a piece of strudel and koffee," the man said.

"*Auf wiedersehen.*" Pyotr walked to the front. He passed Gretta's stare and went out the door.

*Chapter Twenty-Five*

# 2015 - Chicago

The ambulance arrived. Its siren wound down. A blue and white and two other cars soon joined the flashing red lights. Detectives stepped out of their vehicles. Billy Dee stood with the paramedics who had Melissa on a stretcher.

"You see what happened?" Detective Steve Majuski flashed his badge.

Billy Dee nodded. "Yeah, I was about twenty-five feet from her."

Out of the corner of his eye, Billy Dee saw the other detective circle around him.

"He's packing," the other detective yelled, and leapt at Billy Dee. The detective's shoulder crashed into his side. He missed falling on the stretcher and landed on the asphalt. As hands grabbed at him, all he could get out was "Cop." How much time passed, he didn't know. He found himself sitting with his back to the building. Someone had unbuttoned his shirt.

"Does it hurt when I touch here?" the paramedic asked.

Pain shot through him. "Hell yeah. What happened?" Billy Dee asked, his teeth clenched.

"Detective Leap-frog fucked up. He saw you were carrying and came to the wrong conclusion. My partner and

I moved you. You may have a busted rib. Does it hurt to take a breath?"

He inhaled and triggered a coughing fit. His hand went to his side. "Jesus." He looked around. "Where's Melissa?"

"She was taken to Advocate Illinois Masonic. Detective Majuski stayed. He figured you wouldn't want to talk to his partner."

That would have brought a smile if his side weren't aching. "You got that right. What district are these guys from?"

The paramedic looked over. "Hell if I know. Logically they should be from Central, which is down the street, but..."

"Amen to that." He winced in pain.

Majuski stepped toward them. "All right if I talk to him?" he asked the paramedic.

"Sure, just waiting for another ambulance." He moved out of earshot.

"Sorry about my new partner," Majuski began. "He was out on medical and only been back a week."

Billy Dee didn't reply for a few seconds. "What was his problem?"

Majuski pointed to his head. "He's seen too much trauma. What the fuck, it's in our line of work. Rumor has it his last partner was shot. Don't know how."

"You guys out of Central?"

Majuski gave a confused look. "Central?"

"The old Area 6 violent crimes."

"I know what Central is." He looked around and moved closer. "We're out of the Superintendent's office. I can't talk about it."

"You're what? I've been on the force for forty years, I never heard of such a unit."

"That's because we're not in any directory. We're special ops. Here's my badge again."

He examined the star that had Chicago Police inscribed

in the center. It looked real. "Okay, you're a cop. What does your unit have to do with this?"

He knelt so that he was on the same level as Billy Dee. "The long and short of it is, there's a theory the shooting had something to do with that baseball guy, Rakow."

"Hmm, this is crazy. Why do you think so?"

He stood up. "Can't tell you. Did you get a look at the car?"

"You know, Majuski, for the time being the only one I'm talking to is my captain. He'll fill you in." He motioned for the paramedic. "Help me up."

The medic came over. "Where do you think you're going?"

"To my car," Billy Dee said. "I don't have the time to wait."

Majuski blocked his way. "Hey, this is an investigation, and I'm not through."

"Sure you are. You just didn't know it. Get out of my way."

Despite the pain, Billy Dee drew himself to his full height. The two men stared at each other for seconds, then Majuski let him pass.

"This isn' t the end of it," the detective said.

"I'll let the superintendent know you send your regards." Billy Dee limped to his Chrysler. "Shit this hurts." He lowered himself into the driver's seat, and fumbled for the keys. He heard Majuski call out to Pat. He looked into the side view mirror and saw the bar owner walk back to the bar. He didn't have to worry about him.

# Chapter Twenty-Six

# 1975 - Chicago

The light to cross Division and State was red. It didn't matter. At four in the morning, the street was Jack's. Even the touristy horse-drawn carriages were gone. His pace was quick. He wanted space between the hotel and him. Most of all, he wanted time to think. He walked south for three or four blocks and found himself on Rush Street. Stragglers left over from late-night partying staggered from the sidewalk and into the street. A young man in tight pants and fancy shirt and a woman wearing a revealing blouse and high heel boots fell out of the disco called Faces. Neon signs mounted on buildings were ablaze. One had a silhouette of a high kicking dancing girl beckoning patrons to the Club Alabam. There were two men by the curb who caught a smoke. They wore dark suits and had a striking resemblance to Mr. Castellini or whatever his real name was. He quickened his pace. He walked passed a darkened Mr. Kelly's. He stopped for a moment and peered into the window. His father had taken him when he was a teenager to see the comedian Godfrey Cambridge and the jazz pianist Bobby Short. The place was shuttered. There were no people, tables, or chairs, only an empty room. He noticed a sign on the door thanking everyone for their support through the years. Damn, he didn't know Mr. Kelly's had closed for good.

He could use a cigarette. Baseball players weren't supposed to smoke, at least not on camera. What would the public think? Jesus. Thank God the press stuck mostly to what occurred on the field. He tapped his pockets for a hidden pack. No such luck. He must have left his smokes in the room. He felt his pockets again for his cigarette lighter. Shit. What if he left that too? So what, anyone could have a lighter, even Linzie. He couldn't let go of the thought. It was like throwing a curve ball knowing he should have thrown an inside fastball. The batter would hit it out of the park.

It was his dream to play in the World Series, much less to be the starting pitcher. Long after the money and the cheers, his name would be forever in the box score. He lost out the first time in Minnesota. He had to pitch.

As long as nothing of his was found in the room, everything else was, what's the word lawyers use? Circum... circumstantial, that was it. The photos could have been doctored. Linzie and her so- called husband's story were their words against his. He'd take his chances. He turned back to the Ambassador West.

The doorman who had greeted him earlier had his back to him as Jack went through the sliding glass doors. He took the elevator to the lobby. The cleaning staff was busy vacuuming the carpet. Others cleaned tables preparing to open the restaurant across from check-in for early breakfast. He walked around the corner to the guest elevators. This time, the arrival sound of the car was soft and pleasant. He got in and punched 10.

In seconds he was whooshed to the floor. He turned into the corridor and saw a room service cart by 1007. Breakfast this early and for who? He picked up a newspaper left in front of another door. He peered over the paper and saw a woman dressed in the hotel uniform knock. He went closer.

She rang the doorbell. He heard her call out, "Room service." She pushed the door open and went in with a tray.

He was about fifty feet away. He edged closer. A moment later he heard an ear-splitting scream. He froze for a second, then ran into Linzie's room. The room service woman ran into him as he entered.

Her eyes were wide and she appeared to be in shock.

"Let me help you," he said. "I heard you scream." She calmed a bit and pointed toward the bedroom.

He stepped over the dropped tray and saw Linzie lying on her back naked on the bed. There was a gaping slash around her neck and a knife was stuck in her chest. Blood soaked the covers and smeared the wall.

Now he wanted to run. But the macabre image drew him closer. He fought the urge to puke. "Oh my God." He walked backward out of the bedroom and jumped when he bumped into the woman from room service.

"What the…" He turned. The woman didn't speak. He touched her shoulder. "Don't panic," he said out loud. "Stay here and wait outside in the hall. I'll go downstairs and get help."

He helped her to her cart. She leaned on it and began to sob. "God forgive me," she said over again, and made the sign of the cross.

He ran down the hall. He had to get out of there. Who knew what she'd remember? He hit the Down button and waited. The elevator came. There was another couple in the car. Shit. He gave a weak smile and got in. The elevator stopped on 9, then 7, and lastly 5. Seven people along with their luggage made him step back until he stood next to the couple. Everyone couldn't have early flights. He caught a glimpse of his watch… 5:30. *Don't people sleep, goddamn it?* He kept his gaze at the backs of the people in front. He just wanted to blend in. Another traveler on his way to God knows where. He could feel sweat on his face. He hoped the original couple didn't notice. Were they looking at him? He stared at the digital display above the door. The car finally reached the 11th floor. Everyone stepped off. He followed the couple. The man turned.

"Don't you pitch for Boston?" he asked.

Oh shit. This can't be. Think. Jack paused. "No, you must have me confused with someone else."

The man shook his head. "I could swear…" The woman tugged at his sleeve. "Sorry to bother you," she said. "My husband loves sports and the Red Sox."

"Not a problem," Jack recovered, "it happens a lot."

The couple went toward the restaurant. He heard the man say, "that's got to be Jack Rakow. Wow."

"Let's get breakfast," she said.

He waited a few seconds for the couple to walk over to the maître d' and then walked around the corner to the other bank of elevators. The ride was nonstop.

He stepped out into the street. Sirens sounded in the distance. He watched as two police cars and three fire engines approached the hotel. As they pulled alongside the building, he turned east away from the emergency vehicles and walked toward the lake and the hospital his father was in.

## Chapter Twenty-Seven

# Berlin - 1937

He must get rid of that letter. Throw it in the garbage. Bad enough to pretend to study the German treatment of Jews, but to risk one's life for a woman he barely knew? Crazy. Pyotr walked down the street, replaying the close call he had in the bakery. He came to a corner and stepped into the street. A car nearly crushed him. He jumped back on the curb. Death could come from anywhere. Enough. He patted his pocket. Yes, what he was doing was absurd. It brought more danger than he needed. But he was a man of his word. To be in Berlin was in itself ridiculous. He'd deliver the damn letter, the sooner the better. He took out his tourist map. He looked up from the guide and turned 90 degrees. The Brandenburg Gate was four blocks away and towered over the other buildings. The Adlon Hotel was on the other side of the Gate across the Pariser Platz. He moved with the crowd. As he got closer to the hotel, he wondered if he had been followed. He turned his head slightly. No one seemed to pay him attention. He closed his eyes for a second. *Got in himmel, God in Heaven.* What was he doing? What did he know of these kinds of things? He took a breath. Good music required subtleties and depth. They would want to see where he went and to whom he spoke. He might as well make it interesting. Instead of

going directly to the hotel, he decided to be a tourist. He
strolled around the Platz and took in the magnificence of
the Gate. Between each of its six columns hung huge red
Nazi flags. On top was a quadriga statue of the Goddess
of Victory bearing a symbol of peace. He stared at it. He
then retraced his steps toward the hotel. At that hour in the
early evening, there were men in army uniforms strolling
with their girlfriends; others sat on the spacious benches.
He scanned the people as best he could, but didn't notice
anything unusual.

The doorman of the Adlon saluted. "Heil Hitler. May
I help with your valise?" He held the door open.

"Thank you, not at the moment."

"Very well, welcome to the Hotel Adlon. Reception is
through the hall to the right. Libations are down the corridor and to the left." He clicked his heels and resumed his
position at attention.

Pyotr arched his eyebrows. "Libations," he said to himself.
That wouldn't have happened at the Hotel Bristol in Warsaw.
"Thank you again." He entered the marble hall. There was
a crowd of uniformed men. Some wore the khaki of the
Wehrmacht and others wore black with an SS pin on their
coat lapels. The women on their arms were in formal gowns.
He went back to the doorman.

"On second thought, would you be kind enough to check
my bag?"

"Of course." The doorman again saluted and with German
efficiency produced a claim check for the valise. "Enjoy
the evening."

"I will." Pyotr's shoes clicked on the marble floor leading
into the hall. This must be a convention or a dinner. He
was pushed along by the gathering to the Grand Ballroom.

"Champagne, sir?" A waiter handed him a glass.

"Danke," and took a sip. Of course it was delicious.

The doors to the ballroom opened and seven violinists launched into Beethoven's "Emperor's March" followed by a parade of waiters. They carried silver trays loaded with hors d'oeuvres.

"Don't you love these events?" a tall woman with shoulder-length dark hair asked. She was dressed in a silver gown. "One of the Führer's favorite composers."

"Really. Are there others?"

"Wagner and Bruckner."

"Of course. I was just testing," Pyotr said, and snagged pâté on toast off a tray.

"Tonight will be spectacular. Rumor has it the Führer will make a surprise appearance."

"Really? But if it is known, then it won't be a surprise."

The woman's smile never left her face. "Well, eh, not everyone knows."

Pyotr sipped his Champagne. "I will not tell a further soul."

"You are a comedian. It will be our secret." She put her finger to her lips.

"May I get you something to drink?" he asked.

"Of course. I'll wait here."

He searched for the attendee with the Champagne. He found him encircled by several ladies.

"Excuse me," Pyotr said, "May I?"

The women parted to allow him to reach for a glass. The one dressed in green commented on his clothes. "Does he think he is at a market?" she asked. "Ach, a peasant." The other women laughed.

He should have been embarrassed. His clothes were shabby compared to the tailor-made uniforms and slinky gowns.

"Excuse my appearance, fräulein," he said, "but I travel in circles where it is best to blend with the people and not stand out. We all do our duty for the Reich. Heil Hitler."

He couldn't believe he had come up with the line. The

women stood open-mouthed and the face of the one dressed in green turned red.

"Mein herr, I am sorry to have caused you discomfort. It was wrong of me and I apologize. We all believe in helping Germany. Heil Hitler."

"*Entschuldigung akzeptiert,* apology accepted. Enjoy the evening."

"One moment, please, can I introduce you to my friend Major Farber. He's the one in the black jacket talking to General Kurtz behind us."

Pyotr felt as if he had been kicked in the stomach. That couldn't be the same Farber from the train. He tried not to stare but the major had his back to him. He turned to the woman in green. "I'm sure it would be an honor, but they are in conversation, and I wouldn't want to disturb. Besides, my guest is waiting for her Champagne." Pyotr pointed in her direction.

"Very well." The woman in green held out her hand. "Nice to have met you Herr…"

"The same for me." He shook her hand, clicked his heels, and with all the fortitude he had left made his way to find the woman in silver.

## Chapter Twenty-Eight

# 2015 - Chicago

Billy Dee peeled out of the bar's parking lot and onto Belmont. Something was not right with that Majuski fellow. His ID and badge appeared authentic, but his story? What secret group worked out of the Superintendent's office? *Hmm.* He drove east past his police station. Where was he going? His thoughts flashed to Majuski's partner, the idiot who tackled him. Someone said he went to Illinois Masonic. Shit, he had to get to Melissa at the hospital.

He drove to Halsted and turned right. Even though he had no siren or flashing lights, he blared his horn and went through stoplights and signs. He stopped counting the traffic violations. He picked up his phone and added one more.

"Sarge, this is Billy Dee."

He had to move the phone from his ear as Flynn yelled. "Where the hell are you? We got a call of a shooting up the street."

"Listen, Sarge, I know about the shooting. I was there."

"You were? What the fuck were you—"

"Damn it, I'm calling you because the mess with Rakow and this shooting may be connected."

"What? How?"

Billy Dee sighed. "I'm not sure. It's a feeling."

"A feeling? Are you nuts?"

"Sarge, don't go crazy on me. I need a favor." He pulled the phone away from his ear again as his sergeant ranted.

"Stop shouting and listen, damn it. Can you look in Personnel for a Detective Majuski?

"Who?"

"Common spelling M-A-J-U-S-K-I. Don't know his first name. The badge number went something like 475. I'm drawing a blank on the rest."

"Anything else and why?"

"Yeah. Does the Superintendent have an investigation unit that works out of his office?"

"What's this about, Billy Dee?"

"Just do it, Sarge. Call me back when you find something." He pushed End, dropped the phone on the seat, then made a hard right into the hospital's parking lot.

## Chapter Twenty-Nine

# 1975 - Chicago

"May I help you?" A woman at the reception desk of Northwestern Memorial looked him over.

Jack had never liked hospitals. The antiseptic smell of them was unnatural. He took a quick look around and in a controlled voice asked directions to Intensive Care.

"Third elevator on the left, elevator D. Take it to the fourth floor."

"Thanks." He took three steps that way.

"Excuse me, sir, are you visiting a patient?"

He stopped and again checked whether anyone was in earshot. He returned to the counter. "My father...eh, Peter Rakow."

"Could you spell the last name?"

"Really? R-A-K-O-W."

"Thank you." She buried her head in a binder. "Rakow, right?"

"Yes."

"He's on six. Take Elevator F. It will be on your right and down the hall."

"Is that Intensive Care?"

The woman had turned her back and was busy with an orderly. He thought of asking again, but then shrugged. *What the fuck does it matter?* He walked briskly since "down the hall" meant two long corridors. He arrived at the elevator along with a group of young nurses and doctors in their blue scrubs.

"Quite a crowd," he said to one of the nurses next to him.

She gave him a glance then said, "Shift change. Hospitals run twenty-four hours a day."

"Oh." He looked at his watch…5:50 a.m. Jesus.

The sixth floor had signs posted with arrows directing people to pulmonary, cardio, and radiology. Where the hell was intensive care? He decided to follow cardio.

Individual patient rooms surrounded the nurse's station. Three staff workers sat behind the desk and chatted over their coffee and medical charts. There was music coming from a portable radio near one of them.

"Excuse me," Jack said, "Can you tell me where I can find Peter Rakow?"

The one with short dark hair looked up. The name Susan was embroidered on her uniform. "Who? Is he a patient?"

"Yeah, yes he is. He was in intensive care last night. I was told he had a stroke."

The women talked among themselves while opening several folders. "Who told you he was in intensive care?" Susan asked.

He stared at her and took a breath. "I don't know. She didn't introduce herself. She told me my father had a stroke." Susan went back to the binders. "Wait, " he said, "she also said he was in a coma."

"Coma! He wouldn't be on this floor."

"Where would he be, then?"

" Intensive, long term, third floor."

"You're sure?"

Susan looked away but gestured to wait. The music from the radio stopped playing. Jack heard a male voice report the news. "A woman was discovered stabbed to death in her room at the Ambassador West Hotel on Chicago's Gold Coast."

"That's terrible," Susan said. "Wow, it's only a few blocks away. Must have been a distraught husband or a trick that got nasty." The other nurses shook their head in agreement. "At least she died in a ritzy place," she said. The others laughed.

Jack backed away toward the elevator. His hand shook as he pressed the Down button. Time, just time… he had to get out. His life had turned upside down. Some crazy mobster or whoever had put the squeeze on him to throw a game. He was seen in Linzie's room. Who knows whether that crazy motherfucker, Castellini, was waiting for him on the third floor?

*Sorry, Dad, something's come up.* He snuck a look at the nurses. They seemed to be going about their business. He felt nauseated. His stomach gurgled. *Dad, you'll understand. You always had my back, and I…well I thought that was the way it was supposed to be.* He felt his eyes get blurry and wiped away tears. Where the hell is the damn elevator? He pressed the Down button again. Everything will be all right. That was his dad's favorite line. Didn't matter what the crisis. "It vill be okay," he'd say. He was usually right.

Jack bowed his head for a second or so and then looked at the floor indicator. Finally. The door slid open and he stepped inside. He stared at the panel, hesitated, then pressed 1.

## Chapter Thirty

# Berlin - 1937

Pyotr picked his way through the crowd to where he had left the woman in silver. It seemed that all of the Nazi elite had come to this event. The air filled with perfume mixed with the scent of cigars.

"There you are," he said, "so many people. Here is your Champagne."

"*Danke*, I was beginning to worry. Did you know those ladies?"

"Ladies? Not in the least."

"But you had a conversation."

"I...eh, yes, I had to ask them to move so that I could get your drink."

She gripped her Champagne.

"You were able to see?" he asked.

She took a sip. "I was concerned you wouldn't return."

"Why?"

She laughed. "You don't know?"

"I'm at a loss. Please..."

A change came over the room. He noticed despite the din of conversation that the several violinists stopped playing. He looked toward the back. A whole orchestra had lined up. They had their bows high in the air like rifles on parade. Upon a signal, the music of Beethoven's last movement of his "Third Symphony" exploded as they trooped toward the entrance of the Grand Ballroom.

"You were saying?" he asked.

She nimbly put her hand on the elbow of his sleeve. "Let's not rush."

She held onto him as the crowd moved toward the ballroom. She smiled at the men and nodded at the women.

"What are you doing?" Pyotr asked. "Who are you? Everyone is taking their places at the tables."

"I know," she said. "Did you forget you don't have a seat?"

He could feel a drop of sweat start at his hairline and begin to descend down his face. He reached for a handkerchief to wipe the moisture. "How did you…"

"I need to go to the ladies' room. I'm sure nature is sending you the same signal. We'll meet at the hall's entrance where we first came in. Let's say in five minutes. It takes women a little longer."

He watched her walk away. What to think? Most of the people had filed into the ballroom. The uniformed guards closed the doors. Beethoven's Symphony could no longer be heard. He checked his watch. A minute had gone by. The men's bathroom was off the middle of the hall area where the hors d'oeuvres had been served. Most likely out of the sight lines of the guards. There wasn't much choice. If he stayed, he would be found out. This woman offered a chance he had to take. He followed her instructions.

Several people were cleaning the area as Pyotr left the bathroom and went toward the entrance of the hotel. Where the hell was she? He looked at the time. Thirty seconds left. He reprimanded himself for his need to be precise. She did say five minutes. She still had a bit of time. It must be his musical training. Precision and accuracy were the hallmarks of a trained musician. He pulled his sleeve back to check his watch.

"I said five minutes," she said, "and I am on time."

He turned towards her and didn't know what to say. She no longer wore a silver gown, but had changed into a skirt with a brown overcoat.

"Let's go." She placed her hand on his arm.

"Of course." He looked at her. "Where?"

# Chapter Thirty-One

# 2015 - Chicago

Billy Dee walked as fast as he could through the parking lot across the street from the hospital. He put his hand on his right side in the hope the pain from being tackled would subside. A street person dressed in a heavy coat with an unshaven face and hair full of grease came towards him and asked for a dollar. He waved him away and went through the sliding glass doors and into the hospital's reception area. He walked toward a large, elevated, circular desk with the word Information across its front. When he got there, he reached for his wallet and badge. A large black woman with glasses sat behind the console. Her nametag read Danasha Davis. She paid no attention to him. She was talking to someone, but had no phone in her hand. Nor was there anyone else near.

"Excuse me," Billy Dee said.

There was no acknowledgement. He tried again, louder. "Excuse me."

The woman jerked her head and stared at him. "Can't you see I'm talkin'?"

It was only after eyeing her closely that he discovered a well-camouflaged headset.

"Sorry."

She looked up.

He mouthed s-o-r-r-y. She scowled.

He shifted his weight, then leaned on the counter. The reception area even at this time of night was busy. An older woman straggled in with bruises on her face. Two doctors and a nurse passed him; one went out the door and two walked to the elevators. His thoughts were diverted by the ever-sharper ache of his injury.

"Now what can I do for you?"

Billy Dee caught the "you." "What?"

"What do you want?" the receptionist said.

He showed his badge. "A Melissa Stone was brought here by ambulance for gunshot wounds. I need to see her."

She gave him the look his mother and wife gave him when he said something stupid.

"You want to see Melissa Stone. Uh-huh, hold on."

He saw her talk into her hidden microphone. She nodded her head a few times and he thought she said s-h-i-t with the 'i' drawn out.

She then looked in his direction. "Ms. Stone is about to go into surgery."

"I need to talk to her while she's conscious—police business"

"I don't care if you be CPD, KGB, CIA, you ain't goin' up there."

"Hell, you saw my badge."

She gave him an icy stare.

"Listen…"

"What did I just say? Besides, another officer already spoke with her. "

Billy Dee tried to draw himself to his full height, but the pain from his rib cage brought him up short.

"You hurt too or are you playin'?"

He ignored her question. "What officer?"

"Now I'm suppose to know every policeman who come in here? He had a badge like you, dressed like you, but he be white. Said he was with an investigative unit or something like that."

He leaned over the counter as best he could and motioned her to come close. "Ms. Davis, I'm not sure that person is a real cop."

She gulped and her eyes widened. "What you mean?"

"It's a long story, and there isn't time. What floor?"

She blurted "Seven."

He took off toward the elevators as she called security.

## Chapter Thirty-Two

# New York - 1981

The *Los Angeles Times* ran a small story buried on the third page of the sports section. The headline read, "Jack Rakow Returns to the Majors."

The Los Angeles Dodgers called up veteran pitcher Jack Rakow on the eve of their showdown with the hated N.Y. Yankees.

According to Dodger skipper Tommy Lasorda, you can never have enough good pitching. Asked whether Rakow will be used as a starter or in relief, Tommy gave one of his famous shrugs.

"We'll see how it plays out."

The first game of the 1981 World Series would be held in the house Ruth built, Yankee Stadium, home of the Bronx Bombers, New York Yankees. The Dodger team bus pulled up to the gate in the early morning of October 20. Jack, with his baseball gear slung over his shoulder, followed his teammates. He saw a group of reporters huddled by the player's entrance. The stars of the team, Ron Cey, Steve Garvey, Bill Russell walked past. They were greeted by the scribes with "How ya doin'?" and "What a morning!" As Jack got to the entrance, the press surrounded him and yelled a barrage of questions.

"Why'd did ya go to Japan, Jack? What happened in 1975 with Boston? Are you going to run out on your team again?"

Jack smiled and tried to move through the crowd.

"Come on, Rakow, give us something," a reporter yelled.

"Japan was a great experience," Jack said. "Baseball is seen through a different light."

"That's great," another reporter with a black derby said. He stepped close to Jack. "But it explains nothing. What happened to your father?"

The shouting of questions stopped. Everyone seemed to wait for his answer. He stared at the sonofabitch, and had an urge to punch him. Instead, he took a breath and looked directly at the bastard. "My father…"

"Come on, boys, give Jack a little room. He just got here and my God, it's the first game of the World Series." The Dodger public relations man whose nametag read Danny McHugh made a path through the reporters for Jack to follow.

"You owe us, Danny," the black derby yelled as both Jack and the spokesman retreated into the Dodger locker room.

A skinny elderly man who was in charge of equipment led Jack to his locker and gave him a uniform.

"Thanks," Jack said, and held it out in front of him. "Dodger blue."

"That's right. I've handed hundreds of them to guys like you. Good luck."

Jack watched him go. He stared at the uniform for a few seconds, then hung it up.

His manager stopped by and slapped him on the back.

"Glad to have you aboard," he said. "This is a great bunch of fellas and we're all here to do one thing—we're going to beat those New York sonsabitches. After you get settled and change, the pitching coach wants to see you."

"Sure thing, Mr. Lasorda."

"It's Tommy, kid. My dad is Mr. Lasorda."

Jack searched Lasorda's face to see if he meant something more. The manager only smiled.

"Okay, I'll be there in a few minutes."

He reached for his uniform shirt with the number 54. He remembered Don Drysdale, a Dodger legend and sure bet to be in the Hall of Fame, had worn 53. He was in good company. Finally, fortune smiled on him. It had been a long journey after that Chicago night in 1975. He had panicked and left everything, his team, his career, and his father. No major league ball club would touch him after he walked out on Boston. He was the subject of dozens of newspaper articles and editorials wondering what made him do such a strange thing. In Boston, particularly after they lost the World Series, the media simplified the issue. He was worse than Al Capone, and as evil as James Whitey Bulger. He was the example of everything bad about baseball: selfish, greedy, and uncaring. *None of it was true,* he thought to himself. For all of the thousands of words written and spoken never came close to unearthing the reasons he left. He guarded those secrets. Six years was enough time for that crazy sonofabitch Castellini to be long gone and forgotten.

His Dodger uniform looked good. He bent over to lace his spikes when he felt someone nudge him. Jack looked up and saw a man in a brown suit with a newspaper in his hands.

"How ya doin', kid?" The man spoke out of the side of his mouth.

Jack straightened. "Do I know you?"

"You should, but then maybe your memory ain't too good. My memory is real good. I even remember what I had for yesterday's breakfast."

"Sorry, you don't look familiar."

"No, not me. My associate."

"How'd did you get in here?" He motioned with his arm.

The man smiled. "I'm part of da Fourth or maybe da Fifth Estate. Don't remember. A press pass works wonders." He put his paper close to his face. "We'll be watchin', kid. You cost us plenty."

## Chapter Thirty-Three

# Berlin - 1937

"I left my valise with the doorman," Pyotr said as he and the woman strolled toward the doorway.

A uniformed guard with an SS insignia had replaced the stout man who had been there.

"You'll come back for it. I told you the surprise of the evening. Der Führer will be arriving. We must leave before they lock the doors."

"But—"

In an instant, a warning look came over her face that disappeared quickly as they neared the guard. She leaned her head on his shoulder as a lover would.

The guard snapped to attention. "Papiere," he demanded.

The woman slipped her hand in her pocket and presented what looked like diplomatic papers. The guard glanced from the documents to her.

"And him?" he asked.

She smiled and moved close to the guard. She spoke in rapid German.

The official looked from her to him and back to her. He nodded, then smiled.

"Guten abend," he said and opened the door. He saluted, "Heil Hitler," and clicked his heels.

They returned the salute and caught the night's air.

"What was that about?" Pyotr asked. "What did you say to him? Who are you?"

"*Shh*, keep walking. He is watching."

He wanted to turn his head, but did as instructed. They walked toward the Brandenburg Gate.

"My name for your purposes is Ana Bilik. I work in the Czech embassy. Katalyna Paternoskov, the woman you met on the train, is a courier for us. Besides Katalyna, there was someone else on the train who followed you."

Pyotr stopped and looked in all directions.

"We are good at what we do. You will never see who it is; if you do, we've failed."

He had trouble breathing. "I...I..." he stammered.

"It's okay, come. Hitler's motorcade will soon be here."

He followed her lead. They walked to the Tiergarten District. The street was crowded. People were everywhere, even at eleven on a Tuesday night. They walked past nightclubs called the Atrium, Das Beste, Scala, and outdoor cafés. The sounds of hot jazz spilled out onto the street along with Germans who smelled of beer and schnapps.

Ana leaned towards him. "All this will be gone soon. Hitler wants to outlaw jazz, the Charleston, anything to do with America, Jews, and Negroes."

Pyotr stopped to take in the scene.

"Keep going," she said, "do not make eye contact with anyone."

They came to a corner and crossed the street. A café was ahead. The patrons must have moved some of the tables, making it difficult to walk past. Pyotr's side touched someone's arm.

His beer spilled on the table. "*Schwein*," the man shouted.

Pyotr stopped. The middle-age man was red-faced and large. He started to get up.

Ana tugged on Pyotr's sleeve.

"*Warum bist du bei einer hure, Jude bastard?* Why are you with a whore, you Jew bastard?"

There were two women and another man at the table. The woman to the large man's left mopped up the beer.

"It's all right, Heinrich. No harm," she said.

Too late, the man stumbled toward Pyotr and threw a wild punch.

Pyotr stepped back and the man lost his balance.

"Heinrich," the woman screamed. He fell face forward on the sidewalk.

Ana grabbed Pyotr's arm and pulled him away. "We must leave—now."

Pyotr saw blood gushing from his face. There wasn't time to argue. The women rushed to the fallen man. The other man went toward his fallen friend and then yelled, "Halt, come back."

Pyotr and Ana walked at a near run and caught up with the night's crowd. They were two to three blocks away before they heard sirens and saw police cars and ambulances fly down the street.

"We need to get to the other side of the Spree River. There's a safe house on Holzmarktstraße," she said.

"How far is that?"

"About a kilometer."

He looked over his shoulder and saw a car about a block and a half away coming slowly towards them. Its spotlight aimed at the partiers on the sidewalk. He looked ahead. There was no one on the next block. The restaurants and bars ended at the corner.

"We must get off the street," he said, "the police will see us."

"They look seedy," she said.

He checked behind him. The car was closing in. "Here."

He excused themselves to a couple and pushed Ana

toward the club. He pulled open the door and glanced down the street. The car was half a block away. As he stepped in he caught the neon sign on the brick wall. "*Kabarett Musikspaß und mehr.* Music, Fun, and more."

"Got im himmel," he said to himself, "what is this place?"

## Chapter Thirty-Four

# New York -1981

Jack stared into his locker. How could this be happening again? Hadn't he suffered enough? He lost his father. He lost Boston and the World Series. He exiled himself to Japan and hoped for a fresh start. Nothing against the Japanese but the food stank; ball games were like playing college ball, and God damn the loneliness. He didn't speak the language or know the culture. There was no family to write. A minute or so ago he believed his luck had changed—now this. Damn that bitch Linzie. How did she know he'd be in Chicago, at that bar? Sucker must have been written all over him. Now Castellini was back or someone associated with him. He punched the wooden locker door. The blow stung his right hand. "Shit." He shook his sore wrist while he swore at himself.

"You always start out by hitting something?" the pitching coach asked.

Jack had been so involved he hadn't heard the coach call his name.

"Rakow, you better watch what you're doing. Fuck up your hand and you might as well catch the next bus home.

Jack forced a smile. "Sorry about that. I, eh…" He rubbed his hand. "Great entrance, huh?"

The coach took off his Dodger's cap and rubbed his

head. "Whatever that was about—a girl, your momma, money—you put that uniform on, baseball is the only thing on your mind. Got it?"

Jack nodded and picked up his cap and glove. "We're straight, coach. I'll do whatever is asked. I just want one more chance."

"Yeah, kid, that's what everyone in this room wants. You got the chance. What you do with it is up to you. We signed you for only one reason—to beat the Yanks. The muckety-mucks in the front office thought you did well against them. I think numbers only go so far. Your track record for keeping your head in the game ain't pretty. Prove yourself and you may have a job next spring. Otherwise…sayonara."

He let the words sink in. "Well, at least I know where I stand. I appreciate it. This is my third time at the big dance. Nothing will stand in my way. You give me the ball and I'll do the best I can. No excuses."

The coach eyed him for a second or two. "Glad we're on the same page. Don't go punching anything hard unless there's a Yankee uniform on it."

"Gotcha, coach."

"Now get your ass out there."

He shut his locker and walked through the clubhouse. A tunnel led to the dugout. His cleats echoed on the cement. When he got there, several players were on the steps watching and waiting their turn on the diamond. It was a sight that always excited him. Sunlight made the grass brilliantly green against the brown dirt of the infield. He stepped on the field and took in the sight. The cool air made for a great day to play ball. The sounds of a ball hitting a wood bat echoed through the empty stadium. This was his heaven.

"Hey, Rakow, throw me a ball," a player yelled.

He went over and grabbed one. "Sure thing."

"Welcome to Yankee Stadium."

***

Jack remained in the dugout long after the loss of the first game of the World Series. It was late in the afternoon and the field no longer looked inviting. He had gotten his chance to pitch. All those years dreaming of the moment, and he walked the only two batters he faced. He was taken out after that. He threw a total of ten pitches. Ten lousy pitches and only two were strikes. Maybe he didn't have it. It had been six years since he had pitched in the majors—a lifetime.

The coach told him not to worry. "You'll get them tomorrow." Tommy just patted him on the shoulder and trudged toward the tunnel.

Jack lit a cigarette and watched the sun dip below the buildings. After several drags, he threw his smoke to the ground. He got up from the bench and gathered his gear.

"Excuse me, can I have a word with you?"

Jack looked behind him and saw a man in a light raincoat with a pad of paper. He was tall, fortyish, with blond hair and glasses.

"Not in the mood," Jack said. "Besides, who are you?"

"Sorry, most of the players know me as Fred. I'm a sportswriter for the *LA Times* under the byline *Diamond News*."

"Nice to meet you, but I've got nothing to say."

"Hold on, Jack, I think yours is one hell of a story. You're a man of mystery and I think readers want to know what happened. I heard you did Americans proud in the land of the Rising Sun. The Japanese called you *maiti amu*…. mighty arm."

"Yeah, that's right, but their baseball is a little different."

"How so?"

He was about to answer, but then shook his head.

"Come on, let me buy you a drink or dinner. I don't bite."

Jack looked him over. "Nah, really it's okay. Today isn't a good day. I stunk up the place."

"That's why you shouldn't go back to the hotel and dwell on it. New York is a great town and I know just the place. You like Italian?"

Jack's face must have brightened. "Sure, who doesn't?"

"Then Patsy's is where you'll want to go. Hell, you may see Tommy with his man Frank chowing down on pasta."

"Frank?"

"You don't know? Sinatra. He eats there all the time. Lasorda and him are lanzmen, capeesh."

Jack knew he was smiling. "Lanzmen? I haven't heard that in a long time."

"Compadres," Fred threw out, "if that sounds better."

"No, no, I like what you said the first time."

"I'll wait for you outside the players entrance. Don't take a year to shower and change. I'm hungry."

"Not a problem, I didn't do a whole hell of lot of sweating out there today."

Jack went back into the near empty clubhouse. Only the trainer he knew as Joe and Sam the equipment manager were playing cards.

"About time you showed up," Sam said.

"Why? Were you waiting for me?"

"Well, if you want that uniform ready for tomorrow."

Jack looked down at his shirt. "Oh, I'm sorry. Really."

He stripped down, showered, and changed into his street clothes in about ten minutes. He dumped his uniform in the laundry basket. The two men were still playing cards as he walked past.

"Hey, man, I'm sorry I made you wait. It won't happen again," he said.

Sam motioned with his hands to forget about it. "You gave me a chance to take Joe's money. Just keep doing what you're doing."

Joe grunted and stubbed out his cigar.

"Well, goodnight," Jack said.

"Yeah have a nice evening. Oh, I almost forgot." Sam reached into his pocket. "Some guy gave me this," and handed an envelope to him.

Jack took it and headed toward the exit. He opened the letter near the door and took out a piece of notebook paper that was folded in quarters. He unfolded it. "Good work, kid. Just keep doin' da same tomorrah," was written in black letters.

# Chapter Thirty-Five

# 2015 - Chicago

Billy Dee was never fast. As a kid, he was compared to old Sherman Lollar, the White Sox catcher who had to hit the ball to the fence to reach first base. He moved as quickly as he could, all the while feeling pain shoot through his side. He was wheezing when he got to the elevator bank and saw the door sliding shut. "Hold it," he ordered.

Whoever was inside didn't respond. There was about three feet of space before the door closed. He kicked it. The door stopped. It stayed that way for a few seconds. He kicked once more. The door rolled back. Decision made.

"Hey, you could have lost your foot," said a man wearing gray scrubs. Dr. was embroidered next to a name.

Billy Dee gave him a look. "Yeah, I could have," and punched 7.

The elevator clanged and banged its way upward. Its movement stopped somewhere between floors 6 and 7. The light in the car flickered and for a few seconds went dark all together before sputtering on again.

"Shit," Billy Dee said, "this happen often?"

The doctor was huddled in the corner. He looked pale. "I...I," he gulped, "I..." Sweat trickled down his face. He slowly collapsed to the floor.

"Doc, get a hold of yourself. Look, I'm pushing the red

button." Alarm bells went off. "Help is on its way."

The doctor, after much effort, looked up. "Last week… I was…an hour…a fuck'n hour…before I got out. Some damn fool…. kicked the door." He put his head down between his knees and moaned.

Billy Dee turned to study the control panel. "Is there a phone?"

The doctor didn't answer.

"Okay, then." He took out his mobile and dialed the hospital number. He heard the connection being made. "Hello, hello?" Silence. He glanced at his phone and saw the words No Service. "Shit." He stole a look at the doctor. "Hello," he spoke into the phone. "The elevator is stuck between floors 6 and 7." He pretended to listen. "Okay," he said after a minute, "we'll sit tight until you get here."

He put the phone in his pocket and took a step toward the doctor. "They'll be here in a few minutes," he said, "we just have to wait."

The doctor didn't look up. "Liar, you didn't talk to anyone. Nice try."

No sense arguing with the man, especially when he was right. "How long have you worked here?" Billy Dee asked.

The doctor didn't answer.

"Look, we might as well talk. You might feel better."

"I doubt it. I freak out when I'm confined."

"I can see that. What's your specialty?"

The doctor looked up after several seconds. "I'm interning in emergency medicine. This is my third week."

Before he could ask another question, he heard a scream and then a loud thump. He looked up at the ceiling. The car shuddered and the light flickered again. The elevator moved. Within seconds the door opened. There was a mass of people in front. Some were shouting, others reached in and pulled them from the car.

"What's going on?" he asked.

He and the doctor were led to a room near the elevator bank. A large man wearing a badge and a security company patch on his arm talked into a walkie-talkie. "We pulled the two off the car," he said, "they're not injured. I don't know about the other."

"What other?" Billy Dee asked. He moved toward the security man and flashed his police identification.

The man put his walkie-talkie down. "Come with me."

They climbed a flight of stairs to the seventh floor. The elevator door was open. Billy Dee peered into the shaft and saw the top of the car he had been in. A body of a man was sprawled on it.

"What the… What happened?"

The security guard, whose nameplate read McNulty, shrugged and took out a pad from his back pocket. "The nurse on seven said a cop was up there asking about a patient who had come in with gunshots. She told him the patient was about to go into surgery and he had to wait. She left her post and was gone, according to her, no more than five minutes. Alarm bells went off. She had been down the hall and came running back." The guard flipped a page from his notes. "She saw the elevator doors were open, but there was no car. She looked down and saw the same thing you just did."

Billy Dee looked at the body that rested on top of the elevator car. "Holy shit." He turned away. "Where's the nurse?"

The walkie-talkie went off. McNulty listened and said, "Yeah…yes…uh-huh…" and gave him a look. He put his radio down. "You better call for backup. We can't find the patient."

## Chapter Thirty-Six

# Berlin - 1937

The stench of stale beer, cigarettes, and something undefined hit Pyotr. The hostess was a woman well past her prime, dressed to show what she once had.

"Velcome," she said, "a table or a booth in the private section?"

He turned to Ana and glanced back at the door they just entered.

"How private is the booth?" he asked.

"Very."

"Good, then a booth." Ana nodded.

"Ten Reichsmarks."

"What?"

The hostess nodded toward the door. "Thirty und you will enjoy your pleasures in peace."

Ana reached into her purse and paid. The hostess took out a small flashlight and led them up two flights of stairs. "You are booth 47. Hans and Frieda will take care of you. If you like, there are showers at the end of the hall. Zey are not private." She pulled back the curtain and motioned for them to enter. She shined her light at a wall. "There are hooks to hang your clothes or whatever you'd like. Enjoy. The show starts in a few minutes. Pull this cord and you'll be able to see the stage."

The booth had two small tables with lantern-like lights and a dark-colored, very large curved couch. He stepped in and felt something sticky on the sole of his shoe. He hesitated but Ana gently pushed him forward.

The hostess left and pulled the curtain closed.

"We have no choice," Ana whispered. "It is too dangerous outside."

He moved toward the end of the couch and used his fingers to brush his seat.

"You look like a blind man," she said with a nervous laugh. "What's the difference…sit."

He sat at the edge of the couch. "God knows what went on in here."

"Oh, I think He knows. Pyotr, I have no intention of doing any of that, but we might as well be comfortable."

He glanced at her. His shoulders relaxed. He reached into his pocket for cigarettes. "You want?"

She nodded.

This time his lighter worked. He lit hers, then his. "It's funny," he said, "I've never looked at another woman. My wife and I are happy together. We have a son. I got on a train this morning and met Katalyna. She is, or was… I don't know. My wife is a good person, simple in her wants, content. But Katalyna, my God, even my students are nothing like her." The tip of his cigarette glowed as he inhaled. "And now…you. In a place…" He looked around. "Crazy, the world is mad."

"We must keep our sanity," she said, "or we'll be swept up and drowned." She moved a little closer to him, but left a few meters of space.

"Shall I pull the cord for the show?" he asked.

She smiled but before she answered, the curtain to the booth was pulled back. Two people stood in the entranceway. One was male who was tall and muscular and wore only an open shirt that went below his waist and sandals. The woman had shoulder-length hair and was dressed the same.

"Guten abend, my name is Frieda and this is Hans." She looked at Ana. "Now, who wants to enjoy whom?" Frieda stepped toward her.

## Chapter Thirty-Seven

# 2015 - Chicago

McNulty's face paled. "What do you mean, you can't find the patient?" he shouted into the walkie-talkie.

"Negative," the answer came. "We've checked the seventh floor and she hasn't been located."

"This beats all," Billy Dee said. "Is Melissa missing post-op or pre-op?"

McNulty drew a blank and was about to push the talk button. His thumb moved away from the switch. "Who's Melissa?"

"Your patient, Melissa Stone. She was brought in with gunshot wounds. She's in her late twenties, early thirties. The woman at information told me she was about to have surgery."

The officer looked puzzled. "Give me an ID on the missing person," he said into the radio.

A few minutes later the two-way came to life. "Female, 105 lbs., 32, gunshot wound, last name S-T-O-N-E, first name M-E-L-I-S-S-A."

"Let's go to recovery," Billy Dee said. The hall way was crowded. There were two doctors running with their stethoscopes swinging from side to side. A nurse was behind them. Three security people along with fire fighters and police were also rushing toward the open elevator shaft. Billy Dee recognized several white-shirted officers.

McNulty steered Billy Dee to another corridor and away from the commotion.

"The operating room and recovery are down here," he said.

They moved quickly. Emergency buzzers and lights flicked on and off. McNulty took out his pass card and swiped it to open the door. Billy Dee followed him to the nurse's station. He was introduced as a police officer to Linda Callen, the head nurse.

"Here's the paperwork on her. She was definitely brought here. She was being prepped and then…"

"Then what?" Billy Dee asked.

"Well, she was on a gurney and should have been brought into the operating room."

"And?"

"There was another patient. She had a similar name, age, and the patient ID number's last two digits were inverted from Ms. Stone's. That was the person wheeled in for surgery."

He looked at McNulty. "I'm not following?"

"I think what Nurse Callen is saying is that transport took Melissa somewhere else."

She nodded.

"Where?" Billy Dee asked.

The nurse looked at them and her eyes welled. "I think…I… eh… best guess is transport took her to the morgue."

The pain in Billy Dee's side seared through his body. The recovery room began to spin.

"The morgue? You took Melissa to the goddamn morgue?" He felt himself stumble and reached out for the nurse's desk to steady himself. McNulty and Nurse Callen grabbed him before he fell.

"I'm all right. I'm not going to fall," he said and wiped sweat off his face.

"You don't look good," Callen said.

He took a breath and rubbed his side. "Give me a minute."

"Maybe you should have a doctor examine you?"

"I'm okay, really. I don't want to go to the morgue before my time."

"That's not fair, Officer. This is a good hospital. We save lots of lives, but we're human and mistakes are made."

"I can use some water."

Callen walked over to the water cooler and got him a plastic cup.

He gulped it. "Better," and put the container down. "How do we find her?"

When he woke up, he discovered himself lying on a gurney in the emergency room trying to focus on the three people around him. He recognized Callen and McNulty. The third person looked familiar, but he couldn't place him.

"What happened?" he asked.

"You passed out," Callen said. "You have a busted rib and should take it easy. The doctor gave you morphine for the pain. How are you feeling?"

He looked at the IV attached to his hand. "How long have I been here?"

"A couple of hours."

"Hours? I've been… Oh shit. What about Melissa?" He struggled to sit up.

"We found her," McNulty answered.

"You did? Is she…is she alive?"

"Yeah, she is. They rushed her to County. Probably the best place to treat gunshot wounds."

He leaned back on his pillow. "Great. Okay. I need to get out of here." He saw Callen and McNulty look at each other. The third person took a step towards him. Billy Dee raised himself slightly and took a good look.

"Majuski? What the hell are you doing here?"

## Chapter Thirty-Eight

# New York - 1981

The night air was chilly. From the time Jack left the dugout the temperature must have dropped ten degrees. He turned up the collar of his spring jacket and walked past Fred who was in his car.

"Hey, Rakow, where the hell you going?"

Jack turned and saw the reporter lean out his window. "I don't know."

"Did you forget dinner? I'm starving."

Jack shrugged and kept walking.

"Hey, I've been waiting for you. Remember, Patsy's, I-t-a-l-i-a-n?"

He waved him off. He heard the start of a car engine. Within a minute, Fred paced him. His window was rolled down and his head and shoulder hung out the car window, all the while talking. "Jack, you're killing me. Stop. Get in, we'll have dinner for God's sake. This looks terrible."

Jack kept walking.

"*Kin du sterben mit fun du make.* You *mamzer*."

Jack stopped and stepped toward the car. "What did you say?"

"What do you mean, what did I say? I've been asking you to get in the car, damn it, and go to dinner."

"No, no, you said something else. It was Yiddish and it wasn't a compliment."

"So *du farshtyn Yiddish?*"

"Yeah, it's been awhile, but I understand. My parents spoke it all the time." Even in the semidarkness, Jack could see the reporter's face redden.

"*Take.* See, Jack, you're even more interesting. Come on, get in, It's only a meal."

"Another time, Fred. I promise, just not tonight."

The reporter let out a sigh. "Okay, *boychik*, you win, but I'm going to hold you to your word."

"You'll get your story," he said and stepped away from the curb. He watched Fred pull away and drive down the street.

Jack reached into his coat pocket and took out the envelope with the note. He reread it. *I can't run the rest of my life. It has to stop.* He thought of going back to the clubhouse. Did Sam know the person who gave him this letter? To have the trainer on the payroll would make fixing games easy. He took a breath and began to walk toward the subway. He put both back in his jacket, and kept his hand there for warmth. This wasn't 1919 and the Chicago Black Sox. If they had Sam in their pocket, they wouldn't need him. His fingers brushed the note. Linzie died over this. Did he forget? Bastards. He reached the train station and asked the ticket agent which train to the upper west side of Manhattan.

"B or D, which ever gets here first," he said.

He walked down the stairs to the platform. Sam did nothing unusual. Ball players got notes all the time. Screwing around and athletes went together like a baseball and glove. He was getting ahead of himself. Most likely it happened the way Sam said. Someone handed the envelope to him.

## Chapter Thirty-Nine

# Berlin - 1937

Pyotr saw the outline of Frieda's breasts as she stepped toward Ana.

Hans remained in the entryway and leered in his direction. "*Mein herr,*" he said, " *guten Deutschen schwänze interessieren?*"

Ana raised her palm. "Stop, please."

Frieda's unbuttoned shirt rested off her shoulders, exposing her round breasts.

"*Was hast du gesagt?* You do not like? I promise you will enjoy very much."

She glanced at Hans and then Pyotr. "Oh I understand. Your friend is shy," she said to Ana. "You did not know he likes *Deutschen schwänze*? Hans is very good and he will be gentle." She touched Ana's arm.

Ana recoiled and leaned toward Pyotr "Really, please, we just want to be by ourselves." She looked at Pyotr and then at Frieda.

Frieda knelt on the floor by Ana. Her hands rested on Ana's ankles. "It is a new world," Frieda said, "love and sex is to be shared. We of the Aryan race must expose our beauty and give of ourselves. It is our duty." Her hands moved up Ana's legs to below her thighs. If you would rather, I will ready you for Hans, then your friend can partake of my

pleasures. We will make Germany and our Führer proud."
She let her shirt fall off her body.

Pyotr gasped. He had not seen a naked woman other
than his wife. The first time was on their wedding night.

Pyotr's voice shook. " Eh… Fräulein… *wir danken Ihnen
für ihre Bereitshaft… zu teilen.* We thank you for your will-
ingness…to share." He paused and his voice became stronger.
"It is the right thing to do in these times, but," he looked at
Ana, "she is more than enough for me."

Frieda stood within four feet of Pyotr. She rubbed her
breasts with her hands and thrust her upper body towards
him.

"*Sie würden diese für sie aufgeben?*"

He felt sweat roll down the side of his face. "Yes, I would
give those up for her."

Frieda turned to Hans. "They are in love, Hans. Can
you believe it? Love? Ha."

Hans came towards her and placed his arm around her.
He kissed her breasts and then her mouth. His hand grabbed
her ass.

"Yes, Hans, let's show them how to love." Frieda removed
his shirt.

Pyotr jumped from the couch. "Please, enough. How
much do you want to leave?"

Frieda gently pushed her partner away. "You want to give
us money?" She said. Her eyes glared at Pyotr.

"If that is what it takes… yes."

"You think money buys everything? That is what *Juden*
think. Are you a Jew? I know it is rare for Jews to be tall
and blond. I've heard some masquerade as one of us, as an
Aryan, and try to fool us. But there is one way to find out,
mein herr. One special way." She nodded at Hans.

Ana flew off the couch. She wrapped her arms around
Hans and ran her fingernails down his back. As he bent

down to kiss her, she slammed her knee into his balls. "Run," she screamed.

Pyotr grabbed Frieda and threw her on the couch.

They ran down the darkened hall.

***

Pyotr saw a sliver of light some fifteen meters away. Ana took his arm and pointed.

"Can you see anything?" she asked.

"No, *shh*. You're too loud."

"No one can hear us with the grunts and squeals coming from all these closed-off booths."

"What will happen if we are caught?" he asked. "I saw horrible things at the border."

"You don't want to find out," she said.

They held onto each other and moved toward the light.

"Pyotr," she whispered, "I should have asked before, but the letter..."

He stopped. "Yes?"

"On the train, Katalyna gave you an envelope. Do you have it?"

She squeezed his hand, but he didn't answer.

He looked around, trying to figure out where they were, but all was blackness. He shut his eyes. They had climbed two flights of stairs when they were shown their space by that made-up hostess. She had led them down a long and wide hallway...possibly one hundred meters, and it wound around in a semicircle. Where were the stairs?

A shrill scream echoed off the walls. Ana tugged his sleeve. He glanced behind. The unmistakable sound of pounding footsteps was coming towards them. He pulled Ana away from the light.

"*Jüdischen Schweine laufen lose.*"

They froze. It was Hans and he wasn't far away.

"*Psst*, in here," a man's whispered voice instructed. He motioned, then grabbed Pyotr's coat. Pyotr dragged Ana with him.

"You two must be the Jewish pigs our Hansel is screaming about."

In the dim light of the alcove, Pyotr could make out a man with a thin mustache and dark hair combed back. A Clark Gable-like figure who wore an ascot, a dark smoking jacket, and no pants.

Before Pyotr could answer, he heard Hans and Frieda outside the booth. The man pointed to a place away from the curtain and on the other side of the couch.

"Rudy, it is too quiet in there," Pyotr heard Hans say. "Is Gretta not up to it? Or are you entertaining someone else?" Hans pulled the curtain and looked.

Rudy lit a cigarette and offered a drag.

"No, not now," Hans said, "Two fuckin' Jews tried to kill me and Frieda. They must still be on the floor or maybe upstairs."

A female voice came from the couch. "Rudy, honey, what are you doing?"

Rudy put on his practiced grin. "Love calls, Hans. Good luck on finding those Jew vermin. They couldn't have gotten far especially dressed or as undressed as you."

Hans looked down. "I am a fine specimen and so is Frieda. Isn't that so, Rudy? We Aryans are not ashamed of our bodies. Shit, I'll kill them both with my hands."

"The lights will go on shortly when the downstairs show is over. I'm sure you will find them." He dragged the curtain shut and stepped toward the couch. He motioned for Pyotr and Ana to stay where they were as they all listened to the fading footsteps of their pursuers.

A minute or two ticked by before Pyotr and Ana got up from behind the couch. "I can't thank you enough," Pyotr said. "I'm…" he glanced at Ana, "we're so…"

Rudy dropped his cigarette on the floor and sat down next to Gretta. "I owned this club once. It was a palace—an intimate place, better than any hotel. We had an orchestra, not that thumping that passes for a band. There was a place to dine and a place for… Well. Now there's always a show with angry men and angry women." He waved his arms to take in the area. "The idea was to make this a refuge from the ugliness of the outside. But…politics." He sighed, and then stood. "Hitler promised so many wonderful things, but they are really bastards and ruin whatever they touch. This place won't last much longer, and God help the rest of the world."

Gretta, who wore a silky robe, brushed her blonde hair from her face, then reached out for Rudy's hand. "*Ach*, you can be so dramatic. It is not so bad. People still enjoy. Yes, this is not what it started out to be, but when the curtain is closed we make our own fun." She smiled. Her robe pulled slightly apart.

Rudy gave her a look and returned to his seat. "You are a delight." He patted her leg.

"All right, to the problem at hand." He looked at his watch. "In about fifteen minutes, the lights will go on. People will be leaving. If you go now, there is darkness. Our friends Hans and Frieda, though, are probably near the entrance. They'll see you. I think if you leave with the crowd you'll have a better chance."

Pyotr looked at Ana. "What do you think?"

"Why are you doing this?" asked Ana.

Rudy smiled. "I don't have much more to lose. I don't care for Jews, or Russians, and I truly dislike the French. The authorities think I'm nuts. Hell, look at me. I'm daring in my dress."

Gretta moved her hand to his lap. "Not so crazy, just ready." She laughed.

Pyotr saw Ana steal a glance at where Gretta's hand rested.

"Well?" Rudy asked.

Ana still hesitated.

Rudy took out another cigarette and lit it. He took a deep drag while giving Ana a long look.

"Okay, there is a locked door underneath the staircase. From there it leads to the alley. If you want the key, it will cost. Being Jews, you must have something of value. Where is it?

Pyotr stepped towards him. "But you just saved…"

"Don't be so surprised. At least I have the decency to ask. If you're caught, they'll just take."

"It's okay," Ana said. "It's the times we live. Rudy took a risk and now he wants his reward."

Pyotr let her words sink in. It took a moment before he said, "All right, Rudy," and reached into his pocket. "Here, you can have it. The lighter is all silver."

Rudy grabbed it and assessed its weight. He then opened the top and flicked the wheel. A flame shot out. "Huh, and it works, very well." He dug into his coat pocket and gave Ana a key.

"How do we know…"

Rudy continued to flick the lighter. "You don't, but all of life is a chance."

"We do as he suggests," Ana said.

"Settled." Rudy pocketed the lighter and then pointed to the Champagne.

Before he touched the bottle, they heard what sounded like glass breaking, and bursts of shrill whistles. Lights were turned on in their alcove and streamed in from the hallway.

"What is happening?" Gretta asked. She pulled her robe tightly around her.

Rudy paused for a moment, then said, "I think our new acquaintances have even more problems. My guess is either the police or the Gestapo. Either way, they're not good for us and worse for them."

*Chapter Forty*

# Los Angeles - 1981

The attitude in the Dodger clubhouse had changed from somber, to cautious optimism, to the smell of victory. The fifth game of the World Series had just ended and they edged the Yankees 2 to 1. After dropping the first two games in New York, they now had won three in a row. They were one game from winning it all.

Jack was all smiles. This was the second game he was used as a relief pitcher in the ninth inning. Both times he shut the Yankees down.

His control stank in New York. Nothing he threw went for strikes. Was it rust or his mind dealing with shadows of his past? But California was different. He felt it in practice. His body was looser and his mind focused. His pitches had zip and accuracy. The ball went where he wanted: high, low, inside, outside. He was his old self. The California sun was good for him. He took in the congratulations from his teammates. It had been a while.

"Hey, Rakow, tomorrow is a travel day before heading to New York. Many of the guys are going to the Strip for a few pops. Come on along," Danny McHugh, the Dodger press spokesman, said. "You've been living like a monk the last week. There can't be that much going on in your hotel room."

He thought about it. After his New York run-in with Fred

of the *L.A. Times* and that note, he had made a decision. He had gone to Danny and asked him to run interference for him with Fred. It seemed to work. He was left alone, at least until the end of the series. As to the other matter of the implied threat, he kept that to himself. He wouldn't go out after a game. He'd go from the ballpark and back to the hotel. He ate from room service and watched movies. It wasn't glamorous, but it kept him out of trouble. He was a winner now. What the hell, there's only so much Chinese food one can eat.

"Sure, great idea, Danny. It'll take me ten minutes to shower and change.

\*\*\*

Traffic was typical LA. The 101 was clogged with cars. Jack rode as Danny's passenger. He would have been swearing and talking to himself but for every second or third car being a convertible with a blonde or other sweet thing. "Jesus, one is better looking than the other. What have I been missing?"

"Put your eyes back, Jack, wait till we get to the Derby."

"Is all of LA like this?"

Danny laughed, "Not all, but lots. They'll do anything if you're famous or near famous. So watch yourself. You can end up being a trophy."

"Imagine that."

The twenty-minute trip took close to an hour.

"That's the Derby," Danny said.

There was a line that stretched almost a block. "All those people want to get into the place?"

"Don't worry about it. We'll have no problems. We're the heroes of LA. Drink it in, Jack. Everyone here has short memories."

The entrance to the Derby was crowded with people. A tall, dark-haired hostess in tight black slacks and white midriff top led them through the crowd to the VIP section. The bar was made of mahogany and there must have been fifty cushioned seats around it. Away from the bar and well-spaced throughout were stylish tables to place drinks on.

"What do you think?" Danny asked.

"Quite a place. What's over there?" Jack pointed to the sectioned-off area adjacent to the floor to ceiling windows.

Danny smiled, "You either get lucky in one of those curtained-off areas or you sign a deal and make a fortune. This is Hollywood, my man. What'cha having?"

The VIP section filled up with people, and he raised his voice. "Scotch."

Danny held up his hand. Seconds later, a twenty-ish looking woman wearing a skimpy black top and short skirt came to them.

"Hi, I'm Carrie. What would you like?"

"What an open question," Danny said.

She smiled. "I mean to drink."

"Of course. I'll have gin and tonic, and for him," he pointed to Jack, "a scotch."

"Neat or rocks?" She smiled what must have been her customary smile. A look of recognition crossed her face. "Are you, I'm not suppose to ask, but I'm a huge baseball fan, Jack Rakow?"

"Sure am."

"Wow, you sure know how to handle those Yanks. That was sorta dumb. I mean..."

"It's okay. I get tongue-tied too."

"Hey, Carrie, over here," Danny said.

She turned toward him and her business smile returned. "Gin and tonic, got it. Bombay or Tanqueray?"

"Oh, baby, what we could do in Bombay."

"Well, we're in LA. I'll get the drinks."

They watched as she went to the bar.

"That's what I mean, Jack. You're the hero today, and I'm, well… Who cares."

"Hey, look at this way, you'll be here after I'm long gone."

"You got a point."

"Hold the fort, Dan, I'm going to the john. Where is it?"

"Behind the bar."

He threaded his way through the crowd of beautiful people. Several he recognized from magazines and TV. He didn't stop to chat. Near the bar, their waitress looked up and stepped towards him.

"I'm glad you got away from your friend," Carrie said.

"Just going to the john."

She smiled and tore the bottom of her note pad. "Here's my number. Call me. I get off about eleven." She flicked some hair from her face. Her breasts almost declared independence from her top.

He crumpled the paper in his hand and stuffed it in his pocket. "Sure," but he had no plans to follow up. No matter how hot she looked.

He did allow himself to imagine her nude as he walked into the empty bathroom. The image vanished. He exhaled and went to the urinal.

"Well, kid, you pitchin' so much better."

The voice startled him. He hadn't heard anyone enter.

"Yeah, to some people you're doin' real real good."

Jack zipped up and turned around. It was the same guy who had greeted him on his first day with the Dodgers. He even wore the same brown hat.

"What the fuck do you want?" Jack said. He was about ten feet from him.

"Ooh, that tone, not good, pitcher boy. Don't expect to go anywhere. It's just you and me until we understand each other."

"What?"

"There's some people on the other side of the door to make sure we're not disturbed. Capeesh?"

Jack moved toward the entrance.

"Don't try it. The boys already have a certain opinion of you, and it's not good. Their idea is to make sure you don't pitch again. I'm more reasonable. I want to see you do your thing. It will make our winnings so much sweeter. Of course, you have to be in the right frame of mind." Without warning, he landed a punch to Jack's midsection, and then his face. He threw a few more blows before Jack sank to the floor. The man stood over him. "Now, do you understand what I'm talkin' about?"

Jack focused on the man's brown leather shoes as he tried to breathe. He didn't answer.

The man kicked him twice in the stomach.

"All right, okay, I understand," Jack said, the words spoken barely above a whisper.

"My hearing isn't what it used to be. Say it again, pitcher boy."

Jack held up his hand and slowly sat up. He stared at his attacker. "You've made your point."

The man reached down to help him.

Jack stared at him. "I'll get up on my own."

"Suit yourself, but remember. This was only a warm-up. One more thing, that girl in Chicago at the Ambassador West, you remember?"

"What about her?"

"She was murdered and there ain't no statute of what-do-you-call-it."

"Hey, wait a fuckin' minute," he said. He used a wall to steady himself. "I had nothin' to do with that."

"We'll see, kid, we'll see. Just keep it in mind when you pitch your next game."

## Chapter Forty-One

# 2015 - Chicago

The moans of the injured and sick could be heard through the thin curtains of the hospital's emergency room. Majuski made himself comfortable on Billy Dee's gurney. "Can I have a minute?" he said to Nurse Callen. The security guard McNulty was next to her. "It won't take long. I'm part of the police investigation. A lot has happened here in the hospital as well as with Ms. Stone."

Callen looked at her watch. "Okay, for a few minutes. A room should be available any time and he's going, like it or not."

"Understood."

"We'll be just outside." She stepped toward the other side of the curtain. McNulty followed.

"Something isn't right," McNulty said to her.

She looked up from her clipboard. "A million things aren't right tonight. Must be a full moon."

"No, listen. All the cops went to the sixth floor. That's where that poor fella landed when he fell or was pushed down the elevator shaft."

"So?"

"I don't know but…"

She waved him off. "We're right here."

McNulty considered what she said. "I suppose." He wiped his face with his hand. "I need a vacation."

"We all do."

Seconds later, Majuski pulled back the curtain and walked towards them. "Thanks," he said. He put his notepad in his pocket.

They watched him go down the hallway and take the stairs.

"I'll check on our patient," Callen said.

\*\*\*

"How you doin', Officer Jackson?" She glanced at the monitor and then his face. His eyes were half shut. He didn't respond.

"Officer Jackson? Billy Dee? Oh shit." She pressed the Code Red button. Bells went off and a voice on the loud-speaker notified personnel.

The intern in charge ran in. He shined a small light at Billy Dee's eyes and asked Callen what happened. He checked the monitor while she gave a brief history and saw the heart rate rising at a rapid rate. "Is he diabetic?"

"I don't know," Callen said. "He has a broken rib and was being treated for the pain."

"Get the glucagon kit."

Callen ran toward the locked medicine cabinet. She yanked out her key ring and fumbled for the right one. Her hands shook. She had worked in emergency medicine for years and was still awed by life's abruptness. Seconds? Minutes? The lock unsnapped and she pulled the drawer. She scoured the various bottles looking rapidly down the rows. *There!* She grabbed the kit.

Billy Dee's heart rate spiked upwards. The doctor ripped the plastic covering and filled the needle with the antidote. He plunged the shot into Billy Dee's arm. Callen stared at the monitor and held her breath while the doctor shined his light at Billy Dee's eyes.

She slowly exhaled. "His rate is coming down. Thank God."

The doctor clicked off his light as Billy Dee blinked.

"Welcome back," the doctor said.

## Chapter Forty-Two

# Berlin - 1937

"*Achtung*. You have five minutes to report downstairs. No one is to stay in the alcoves." Loudspeakers blared on every floor.

"*Achtung*, you have four minutes…"

"Should we go?" Pyotr asked.

Rudy turned to Gretta. "Dear, I'd put something over your robe. The night air will be chilly."

They could hear people running down the hall. Screams came from below.

"*Achtung!* You have three minutes…"

"Why are they counting?" Pyotr asked. "Are there windows, fire escapes?"

Rudy looked up while putting on his pants. "Windows are on the top, three floors above us, and there are no fire escapes. If you jump, it's from the fifth story, and you will die."

Gretta got up from the couch and went to the corner of the alcove. She pressed on the wood and a door opened with a full-length mirror attached. "What should I wear?"

"You're worried about a dress or shoes that match? My God." Pyotr said. He caught a glimpse of hanging dresses, coats, and men's suits. From the reflection the amount of clothes seemed endless. "How deep is that closet?"

Rudy fastened his belt and moved toward Gretta. He dipped down and opened a table drawer.

"Gretta, take the long coat, the brown one with the fur collar. It's toward the back."

She turned towards him with a half- smile.

"*Achtung*, you have one minute. Everyone must be out and downstairs. This is your final warning."

Rudy stood up and stepped toward the closet. He had a pistol in his hand. "*Auf Wiedersehen*."

"What are you doing?" Pyotr said.

"Leaving. You have your means of escape and we have ours. Whether any one of us makes it is up to your God of choice." He pushed Gretta inside. The door shut with a click.

Pyotr rushed over and ran his hand across the wood. "Ana, help. There must be a switch, something."

Her hands swept over the door they had just seen. She found nothing.

"How can this be?" he asked. "We saw the same thing, didn't we? Two people were here and now—"

She put her finger to her mouth. "*Shh*, listen."

The hallway was quiet but for the static hum of the walled speakers. They stared at each other. Neither moved. From below, they heard muffled voices and then cries. Seconds later, *rat-tat-tat, rat-tat-tat.*

"Oh my God...the people." He sank to his knees. He wanted to cry, to shout, but caught himself. He cradled his head in his arms, and then straightened. He went toward the front of the alcove and slowly opened the curtain. He peeked into the hallway. It was empty. A crash came from downstairs. He heard shouted commands, and then he smelled the unmistakable scent of burning wood. He grabbed Ana. "The building is on fire."

"On orders of Reichsführer Heinrich Himmler, this

*schweinestall* of immorality and decadence is to be destroyed. It will no longer stain our German national honor. Heil Hitler."

The announcement boomed through the speakers as wisps of smoke rose from the first to second floor.

Ana stood transfixed. "We must leave," Pyotr shouted. "Ana!" The smoke became thicker. They coughed and wheezed. "Get down on the floor," he said between gulps of air. When she didn't move, he pushed her. "Do you have a handkerchief?"

She didn't respond.

"Ana, we are not going to die. Not here. Let me help you."

She looked at him and shook her head.

He ripped off his tie. "Cover your nose and mouth. He felt heat from the floor. "Ana, now." He seized her arm and pulled her with him. They crawled into the hallway. "Grab my ankle and don't let go. We'll go on our bellies and find the staircase." Smoke poured from the alcoves into the hall. He looked behind and saw fire and a wall of blackness creeping towards them. He used whatever skill he learned in a pioneer Jewish camp to move forward. He didn't know how far he had crawled before he realized his foot was free. She had let go. He looked. She was stretched out several meters behind, panting. "Ana," he screamed.

"I'll...be...al..." she choked.

He crawled over using his elbows and legs and stuck his fingers into her mouth. She wretched and then went into a coughing fit. She pounded the floor with her fist as she gasped for breath.

"We can't wait." He pulled her up. He put his arm around her waist and dragged her.

Through the smoky light he recognized the dark lattice-work of the staircase. It was some twenty meters in front. *Thank God.* "The key, give it to me."

She didn't answer. He held onto her.

"Ana, the staircase we're almost there. Give me the key."

Her eyes widened. There was a whoosh. He looked over and saw the landing consumed in a cloud of black smoke.

"Ana, we can't go back. We can't stay. We must—" The smoke burnt his eyes. He felt his throat close. He was being smothered. He stuck his own fingers down his throat. He wretched and went into a fit of coughing. In his struggle, his hand slipped from her side. She fell. He bent over and then sank to the floor. He cradled her head and tried to shield her from the smoke and flames. "Ana, we don't... have... far..." his voice a raspy whisper. The fire's heat singed his jacket as well as her coat. "The key." He held out his hand. "Ana, it's only...a few more...steps. We'll get inside...and we'll...be safe. Rudy promised."

Ana moved her hand slowly into her coat pocket. Her hand shook. She pulled out the key. "Here, take it," she could barely be heard above the roar of the flames. "Save yourself, Pyotr, go."

A chandelier crashed. Shattered glass flew like crystal missiles. Shards cut his face. He used his sleeve to soak up the blood. In a few more seconds, escape would be impossible. "Ana." He grabbed her arm and pulled, but her body didn't move. He looked up and saw flames coming towards him. "Ana."

He dropped her hand and ran in a crouch toward the staircase and the steel door underneath. He steadied himself and inserted the key. He placed one hand on the hot metal handle and with the other jiggled the lock. *Come on... come on. Got im Himmel.* He didn't need to look back to feel death's breath behind him. He gave the door one more shove and fell in. The door shut.

***

Was he dead? It was pitch black. If he was, why was his hand throbbing? He lifted his arm to his face. It felt sticky. His body hurt, his mouth desperate for water. If he was alive, where was he? That thought caused him to slowly gather his strength and sit.

He cradled his head in his arms, and rocked. In darkness there is no time. He pictured his wife Grunia and his baby Frederyk. What were they doing? Were they out on a Sunday walk? Was it Sunday? He looked up into the nothingness and using his hands, felt around him. There was a floor and behind him a wall. Where was she?

"Ana," he called.

Silence.

He sucked in his breath. Although he had been to *cheder*, Hebrew school, he was not observant by the standard of the day. He kept a kosher home, and the Sabbath, but religion wasn't central to his life. It had always been music. God was an occasional companion.

His lips began to quiver. Out of the depths of his body, he slowly began to recite the Jewish prayer for the dead. "*Yisgadal, vey yisgadash, shmey rabah,*" when he finished he had no tears, only a recognition he had survived.

## Chapter Forty-Three

# Los Angeles - 1981

"Hey, what happened to you? Danny asked. "Did you have a quickie with our waitress? You look like shit."

Jack shook his head. "I'm leaving."

"Are you kidding? The night is young. Some of the other guys will be here in a few."

"That's okay. I'm not feeling great. Must be something I ate or drank. I don't know. I'll get a cab."

"You better be okay for the game. We leave for NYC at eight in the morning. The front office will have my ass if you're not."

"Thanks for your concern. I'll be fine."

Danny got off his chair. "I'll get a taxi for you. Sit tight." He went off to the front.

Jack took a seat. He wrapped his hand around a glass of ice water. He wanted to put it against his stomach. The pain from the punches and kicks was killing him. Everything was a blur. Carrie had to tap him on his shoulder after she served the drinks. He jumped.

"Whoa, are you all right?" she asked.

"Sure, with all the noise, I didn't hear you coming." It was a lame excuse but what the hell, he wasn't feeling sociable.

"Hey, you must be jacked up for the game day after tomorrow. I hope you win."

He heard himself say, "Thanks." He sensed she was still at the table. He let go of the water glass. "I'm fine, really." He looked at her. "My friend is getting a cab for me. I'll be at the hotel." He reached into his pocket and took out a $10 bill along with the crumpled note she gave him earlier. He straightened out the paper and reread her name. "Carrie?" He smiled. "I mean, Carrie. I'll see you around."

"Sure thing." She took the money. "Is this for both drinks?"

It took him a few seconds. "Yeah. Keep the change."

"You mean the fifty cents?"

"Shit. Sorry." He put a couple of bills on the table. "Better?"

Before she answered, Danny came back and put his arm around her waist.

"Hey, darlin'. Your ball player is poopin' out. A cab is waiting out front. Now you got me all to yourself."

She aimed her plastic smile at Danny and gracefully stepped out of his grasp. "Must be my lucky day."

Jack got up and started moving to the front.

"Good luck," she said.

He didn't know whether his "thanks" got swallowed up in the crowd. He elbowed his way out the door.

"Hey, which one is the cab to the hotel?" he asked one of the car hikers.

"*Mi Inglés no es muy bueno,*" he said.

"What? Cab, where...is...my...cab?"

The man had a blank look.

Shit. Jack looked around to speak to someone else. "Anyone know English?"

Before he had a chance to ask, he spotted Fred of the *L.A. Times.* There was no place to hide.

"Hey, if it isn't the Yankee killer, Jack Rakow. Boychik, how ya doin'? You comin' or goin'?" Fred asked.

"Leaving, early flight."

"Spoken like a true Boy Scout. Well, as fortune will have

it, I'm going too. We'll share a taxi."

"Great." Jack took a quick glance. No one was there to save him.

He watched Fred speak to the same valet. The two of them shared a laugh and then the man held out his hand and waved down a taxi.

"*Gracias,*" Jack heard Fred say and saw him hand the man a bill or two. Fred motioned for Jack. "Your chariot is waiting."

"Thanks." Jack got in on the driver's side. Pain shot through his body when he reached to shut the door.

"You all right?" Fred asked. "You look like you've been chewed up and spit out."

"Nah, been a long day."

"Uh-huh." Fred gave him a hard look. "*Ver zenen ir kidingz?*" (Who are you kidding) he said in Yiddish.

Despite the aching, Jack smiled.

"Boychik, one minute you look like you're dead and the next you have a happy face. What gives?"

"You, Fred. When I hear that language, I think back to my parents."

"*Take*, really? Me too. I was maybe ten years old when I came to the U.S."

"So you were born…"

"We lived in Łódź. It was not far from Warsaw. I have a few different birthdays. Birth certificates along with everything else were destroyed in the war. My mother, or the woman who came to be my mother told me I was born in 1937."

He stared at the reporter. "That's quite a story. Were you in the camps? How did you survive?"

"The cab ride isn't long enough even if it's LA traffic. " He paused. "I was very lucky."

## Chapter Forty-Four

# 2015 - Chicago

Billy Dee sensed something bright aimed at his closed eyes. By reflex, his hand went to his side where his gun should have been. It wasn't there; instead he felt his skin. That woke him with a start. There were at least two or three people in scrubs around him. A person wearing a mask pointed a small light at his face.

"Welcome back."

"Where have I been?" Billy Dee asked. The words were slurred and seemed to fall out of his mouth.

"Are you a diabetic?"

He had heard that voice before. He was sure it was recent. Think. It came to him after several seconds. It was that nurse, Callen. The one who screwed up with Melissa. He tried to sit up but he was gently pushed down.

"You need to rest," he heard Callen say.

"Okay, I'll take it easy." He must have grimaced.

"Something wrong?"

"Nah, well, yeah, the last thing I remember was... Jesus, what was his name? Ma... Majuski, he wanted to talk. Where did he go?"

"You mean Officer Majuski?" Callen asked.

This time he did sit up. "Hold on, did he tell you he was an officer? Well, I'm pretty damn sure he ain't."

"Officer Jackson, please. You have a broken rib and you almost went into insulin shock."

"What? How?"

"You are diabetic, aren't you?"

"Diab… No, at least not before I got here. What is going on?"

He saw Callen's face pale. She stared at the doctor.

"You better get Security. Wasn't McNulty here a minute ago?" He wiped some sweat from his face.

Callen ran out of the room.

"Doc, I need my clothes."

"Officer, medically I don't think you should, but I can't stop you. You'll have to sign release forms." He drew a breath. "Lawyers."

"Yeah, I got you. No problem, I'll sign."

∗∗∗

Billy Dee winced as he put on his shirt. Jesus, he could use some more pain- killers. He looked over at the doctor who was busy filling out papers. Probably his discharge forms.

"So let me get this straight," he said, "somehow I went into a diabetic shock after Majuski left."

The doctor nodded. "Yeah, you were almost gone. Nurse Callen found the antidote in time."

"Well, thank her for me."

"She'll be back with Mr. McNulty. You can thank her yourself."

Billy Dee went over to a chair where his personal belong- ings were in a plastic bag. He dressed. The socks and shoes posed a challenge, as he had to bend. He gritted his teeth and finished. He stood and put his hands in his pants pockets. "Hey Doc, what did you do with my phone?"

The doctor turned from his desk. "You'll have to ask

Callen. She may have locked it up with your gun."

"Sure, no problem."

The doctor handed him a clipboard with multiple forms attached. "After you read it, sign by the X."

He skimmed over the pages and signed in several places. "I tell you this," he looked up, "police work is all about doin' the paper and it's for shit. We spend more time on this crap than we do catching bad guys."

The doctor took the papers from him and dropped them on his desk. "Yeah, the irony is with all this documentation we actually expose ourselves to more liability," the doctor sighed, "but it's the way of the world in our attempt to protect all from everything."

"I hear you, Doc."

Callen poked her head inside the room. "Mr., I mean, Officer Jackson, I still think you shouldn't—"

"Too late," Billy Dee said, "I already signed my discharge. Thank you for everything you did."

She blushed. "Ah, well, I'm thankful too." She played with the end of her stethoscope. "Mr. McNulty will be here in a minute or two. It's important you talk to him."

He glanced at his watch. "Sure, but…" He let out a frustrated breath. "Oh, while we're waiting, where's my phone?"

She took a step toward the plastic bag that was on the chair. "It should be in there." She picked it up. The bag was empty. "I don't get it. I put it there myself."

"You did?"

"Yeah, after you passed out, we brought you to the emergency room and I took your phone, and your clothes and bagged them. I then hung the bag in the closet."

McNulty came into the room. "Sorry for the wait. I ran downstairs in the hope I would find Majuski. The security guard and information person weren't helpful. I've alerted the staff in case he's still in the building, but we don't know.

The cops upstairs are busy working on the other case. A sergeant or officer in a white shirt said he'd come by."

"Okay, this situation has gone from bad to real bad. The son of a bitch took my phone. I don't know why or what it means but it can't be good. I need to call my wife and my captain. God only knows what they're thinking."

McNulty reached into his pocket. "You can use mine."

"Thanks, and someone please get my gun."

## Chapter Forty-Five

# Berlin – 1938

Pyotr was led into the courtroom. His blond hair had prematurely turned gray. His jacket was threadbare and hung loosely around his now bony frame. The guard shoved him toward a wooden chair that was below the judge's vacant seat. Two Nazi flags hung on poles on either side of the court's bench.

"*Jude hund*, sit. I don't know why there's a trial. We all know the result," the guard laughed.

Pyotr sat where he was told. The officer took a step back. He didn't blame him. He hadn't been allowed to shower in days. His clothes still reeked of smoke and dried blood. Two months had gone by since he was found at the building and arrested.

***

Was it a day, a week? He didn't know how long he had stayed under the staircase. The men who pried open the metal door must have been startled.

"*Das ist einen mann . Ist er noch am Leben?*" *There's a man. Is he alive?* he heard someone say.

He didn't move. Another asked, "*Was tun Sie? Was ist Ihr name?*"

He felt being jabbed, and opened his eyes. Someone again poked him in the ribs with a rifle.

The uniformed man asked again, "What are you doing? What is your name?"

Pyotr tried to speak. The words stuck in his mouth. He felt himself being lifted.

"*Wasser*, water," he used his remaining strength to say. That was all he remembered. The next time he opened his eyes was in a hospital. His stay there wasn't long. Three days at most. He was treated with typical German efficiency. The doctors and nurses checked on him. He was given food and drink. On the last day, two policemen came. They gave him his old clothes and took him away blindfolded.

\*\*\*

"*Guten nachmittag*, good afternoon," said the man who sat across from Pyotr. "Cigarette?"

Pyotr hesitated, then nodded. His eyes were no longer covered. He glanced at the metal door that had closed behind him. He sat in front of a small wooden table in a large room. Another chair was on the other side. The walls were bare other than a large portrait of the Führer. Pyotr held the front of his coat closely together with his free hand. The chill of the room seeped through.

The man who gave him the smoke wore a black uniform with an SS insignia.

Pyotr inhaled deeply and then coughed. It was the first cigarette he had in weeks. The uniformed man waited until he stopped.

"My name is Captain Heigel. You have been brought to Plötzensee prison. I am giving you this courtesy because you are not German, but a Polish citizen."

Pyotr listened but stared at the ash being formed.

"We know who you are. Your identification card was in your wallet, Dr. Rakowski."

He raised his head and stared at the interrogator. An icy feeling swept through him. He had a sudden urge to tap his pockets. Why hadn't he remembered Katalyna's letter sooner? What happened to it? In the chaos of the fire and the hospital he had forgotten. He would be considered a spy if the bastards found it.

He cleared his throat. "Yes, I am a Polish citizen. I was in Berlin for a conference."

"Conference?"

He struggled to find his voice. "Yes with Dr. Reinhart Gertz."

The Captain tapped his Montblanc fountain pen on a pad of paper. "Gertz is an authority on Juden relations. Is that not so?"

"Yes, he has written extensively on the subject."

"Did you actually meet with him?

He stared at the cigarette smoke swirling above before answering. "I think you already know. I stupidly wanted to see Berlin before the meeting."

The SS captain smiled and scribbled something on his pad. "We'll come back to why you wanted to see Dr. Gertz." He looked up from the paper. His blue eyes had a twinkle. "Berlin is famous for its cabarets. Why did you pick the Kabarett Musikspaß? There are so many others."

Pyotr shivered. There was no good answer. He raised his eyebrows and sighed. "I don't know. It was near the end of the street and…"

"Oh, Dr. Rakowski, a man of your station going into a place like that. *Tsk tsk*. You knew what it was?"

He let go of his coat. "No. The signage said music. I'm a professor. I mean, I've studied music. I thought I'd be listening to…"

The captain laughed. "Oh, that's a good one, Dr. Rakowski. You went there to listen to the music. Who were you with?"

Pyotr shifted his weight and recrossed his legs. The question unnerved him. Should he name Ana? He stared at his interrogator. What do they want to hear?

"Captain Heigel, you have put me in prison for what I don't know. I am a guest in your country—"

The Captain leapt out of his chair and slapped him hard across his face. "Don't be insolent, Dr. Raskowski. You took our hospitality and shit on it. Now, who were you with?"

He rubbed his face and looked wildly around the room. The Captain stood next to him ready to land another blow. "Okay. A young woman," he finally said. "I met her at a café." He put his head down and spoke softly. "She was the one who told me about that…place."

"I see."

"Captain, I am ashamed. I'm a married man."

"Of course, understandable, uh huh." The Captain took his seat. He put his elbows on the table and leaned forward. "You are lying, and we both know it. Doctor, it will go badly for you. I tried to be civil, one gentlemen to another, but…" He looked up at the ceiling. "You came to Berlin to destroy the cabaret. People were killed because of you."

"What? Captain Heigel, I did no such thing. I almost died in that building."

"I will not tolerate your lies," the Captain shouted and knocked the chair over as he got up. He reached into his coat pocket and pulled out a crop. He flicked his wrist and the whip made a whoosh, then *crack* when it struck the table. He stood over the prisoner. "Let's try again, Dr. Raskowski. I want names and details. Germany must be protected from scourges like you. Do you know how many people lost their lives?"

Pyotr looked up.

"Do you care?"

"Captain, I, too, was a victim. I didn't—"

The whip went across his face. "False. You bomb thrower. We have witnesses. Where did you get it?"

## Chapter Forty-Six

# Los Angeles - 1981

Jack pressed his hands together. He did that sometimes out of nervousness.

"You all right, kid?" Fred asked. "What happened to me was a long time ago. I was a baby and then a little boy. It all worked out. I don't remember the bad stuff."

Jack looked out the cab window. "My parents also came from Europe. I was born there in a DP camp."

"No shit."

He turned to Fred. "Yeah, I was five or six when we came to the US. My mother had family in Chicago. They somehow learned she had survived. It took years, but we finally got out."

Fred gave him a long look. He wagged his index finger at him. "Ever since that night in New York, I've watched you. I've asked around, but other than your statistics, you've kept your life hidden. I knew you were born in Germany and raised in Chicago, but that's about it. I bet you even changed your last name."

Jack considered whether to answer, but the cab pulled into the hotel's driveway. "I'll give you this, Fred. My parents were Holocaust survivors. I grew up with the words 'be careful' ringing in my ears. My mother particularly tried to keep me close. 'Don't do too much, Yankeleh, you'll hurt yourself.'"

Fred shook his head in agreement. "Oh boy, isn't that how all of us grew up."

"I don't know. We were the only survivors on the block. My mother's accent stood out."

"So you were ashamed?"

Jack reached for the door handle. "Keep digging Fred. *Zei gezundt*, stay healthy."

He got out of the cab and went into the hotel.

***

Jack didn't notice anything out of place in his room. That was a good sign. He went to the bathroom and took off his shirt. There were red bruises on his body where he had been punched and kicked. He got some ice from the small refrigerator and wrapped it in a washcloth. He turned on the TV, sat down, and iced his sores. He must have drifted off. A noise at the door floated into his consciousness. A few seconds passed before he identified the sound. Someone knocked. He turned the TV down.

"Mr. Rakow? I mean Jack. Hello?"

It was a female voice. He went to the door.

"Jack?"

He waited a second or so, then opened it a crack. A woman with reddish hair and tight jeans looked back at him.

"It's me. Remember the Brown Derby? Carrie?"

He pulled the door wider. "What? Why are you here?"

She stepped toward him. "Your shirt is off and like... wow! Muscles and a six-pack." She took a breath. "Were you expecting me?" She didn't wait for an answer but wrapped her arms around his torso and kissed him hard.

## Chapter Forty-Seven

# Berlin -1938

Pyotr's sessions with Captain Heigel melted one into the other. He remembered each began civilly. Once, in addition to a cigarette, he was given coffee. Heigel stared at him as he took a sip.

"*Gut kaffee?*" he asked.

Pyotr nodded.

"So, Doctor, tell me about your wife."

"Why? She's a good woman, Captain. She keeps the house clean."

"Do you have children?"

He hesitated. Where was Heigel going with this question? He answered,

"Yes, I have a little boy."

"A boy. How nice." Heigel played with his pen while gazing at the ceiling.

"Does your wife know she sleeps with a murderer?"

Pyotr put the cup down. "Herr Captain, it was not I who destroyed the cabaret. I've told you that."

"You did. You also told us the Polish foreign office sent you."

"That is correct."

"We checked with your government. They don't know a thing. They said they've never heard of you."

"What a surprise."

His response was not to the Captain's taste. Pyotr was beaten until he almost passed out.

Another time, perhaps the last, Pyotr was brought in for questioning. Heigel, dressed in his black uniform, did not offer a cigarette or anything else. He looked up from the open file on his desk and leaned forward. The tirade of questions began, but they were the same.

"Who were you with?" the Captain asked. His face was flushed.

"A girl."

"What is her name?"

"I don't know."

Heigel rose from his desk and barked the next question. "Where did you get the material for a bomb? Who helped you?"

"Please, dear God, I've told you I had no bomb."

Heigel grabbed a wooden club from behind his desk. With a swing, he knocked Pyotr out of the chair.

He lay on the floor and drew his knees into his stomach. His arms cradled his head for protection. He heard Heigel breathing heavily. "For the last time, who helped you?"

"Please, Herr Captain, please... It was Himmler. He..."

He peeked through his fingers and saw Heigel swing the club over his head.

"You said Himmler helped you?"

He didn't know what else to say. This was his end. He waited for the blow Seconds ticked by. "Yes, Himmler ordered the destruction," he finally said.

Heigel put the club down. "Get up, Doctor. Sit." He pointed to the chair.

Pyotr had to grab onto the captain's desk in order to stand.

"How was it that you came to know the Reichsführer?"

"I was there when he ordered the cabaret to be destroyed."

Heigel picked up his pen and scribbled a note. "That will be all."

As he was led away, he saw Heigel look up from his desk. He wore a smile and Pyotr's file was closed.

\*\*\*

The courtroom filled with people. Pyotr took a quick glance behind him and saw reporters with their cameras.

"You, *Juden scheisse*, turn around. Let the German public see…"

He heard a ripple of laughter as he tried to ignore their presence.

"The German people want to get a look at you."

He didn't move. Someone grabbed his shoulder and shook him. A man's voice whispered in his ear, "*Jude schwein*, Jew pig. How dare you—"

Pyotr turned. "How dare I what?"

Flash bulbs went off until the guard came over. "Enough, this is still a courtroom, not a cabaret. Sit down." He then stood a few meters from Pyotr.

"The judge will be out soon. You are to stand and answer his questions with a 'yes sir' or 'no sir'. Do you understand?"

Pyotr nodded.

A stocky man dressed in a rumpled dark suit holding papers walked toward Pyotr. The man said something to the guard that made both laugh.

"You," he said, "I am your lawyer. The name is Otto Brach."

Pyotr stared at him. "When did I hire you?"

"Funny. The German legal system allows everyone to be represented. I'm the lucky one who has been assigned your case."

"I see. What am I charged with?"

Brach flipped the papers he held. "*Ach*, here it is. You are charged with *Rassenschande*, race defilement."

"What?"

"Yah, you are accused of being a Jew and having sexual intercourse with a female of the Aryan race."

"Preposterous, I am Polish and did no such thing." He must have raised his voice. The reporters edged closer to him.

"Not so loud." Brach moved closer. "We already know you are a Jew, whether you look like one or not."

Pyotr gulped. What could he argue? "Sexual intercourse?" was all he could say.

Brach put a pair of bifocals on his nose and read further. He placed a finger on a page and read. "Uh-huh, oh my." He looked up at his client, then continued reading.

"What does it say?" Pyotr asked.

"You know what you had done." Brach smirked. "You are quite a Casanova. One was not enough but you had two at a time. Well, the memories will keep you warm at night."

"What are you talking about? I didn't have sex with anyone."

There was a loud knock. Pyotr and his lawyer looked up. The judge, dressed in a crimson robe with black trim, limped across the platform to his seat. He appeared to be in his late fifties. His face was round and reddish in color, as if he were perpetually angry or drunk. He was completely bald. "Prisoner, stand."

Pyotr rose; so did his attorney, Brach.

"Who are you, sir?" The judge asked the lawyer.

"Otto Brach. I will be representing the prisoner."

The judge looked down at some papers and then nodded. "Very good. You are entering a plea of guilty? Yah?"

Brach glanced at Pyotr. "Yes…"

"What are you saying?" Pyotr said. "No! I'm not guilty of anything."

Laughter rippled through the courtroom.

The judge's face reddened. "A Jew not guilty of anything? Now there's a concept at odds with history. You people have plagued society for ages. Germany is learning how to deal with your kind. Do not talk unless I address you. Understood?"

Pyotr fought back the urge to speak. His palms were sweaty and his shoulder twitched.

"Herr Brach, do you wish a hearing?"

Again he gave a quick look at his client. "Yes."

"Very well." The judge turned his attention to another man dressed in a black suit who was seated across the aisle from Brach.

"Herr Schmidt, will the prosecution be ready this afternoon?"

"We are ready now."

"Good. We will have our hearing at 2:00 p.m. Remove the prisoner." He banged his gavel.

The courtroom's decorum dissolved into a babble of voices. Flashbulbs went off as Pyotr was taken away. The guard opened the door that led to the cells. Pyotr looked back and saw Brach talking to the prosecutor. His lawyer had his hand on the prosecutor's shoulder. Both were laughing. The door closed to a chorus of *Jude schwein*.

## Chapter Forty-Eight

# Los Angeles- 1981

The waitress was the last thing Jack desired or had thoughts about. She pushed him inside the room and kicked the door closed. There was a side of him that didn't want any part; the other, well, reacted.

"*Uhm*, you are delicious. When I saw you at the restaurant, I thought wow, you would be…"

"Hold on, ah, Carlie," Jack said, breaking away from her kiss.

"It's Carrie, but that's okay. You'll remember when our night is over."

She ran her hands over his body and planted kisses where her fingers had been. "God, I've never had a major league pitcher," she said, stopping her attack. "Outfielders think they're God's gift, but I don't think so. Let's see what you got."

She went for his belt. "This is worse than a bra, God-damn it."

He looked down. "The buckle interlocks." In a quick motion he undid the clasp.

"All right." she slipped off her jacket, then raised her arms and took off her top. "I didn't think I needed anything underneath."

Her eyes were ablaze as her hands gripped the top of his pants and pulled.

"Look at that. Definitely big league stuff," she said.

He couldn't think of a comeback. She led him to the bedroom and slipped out of her jeans. This was happening too fast. Holy shit, she was gorgeous. She grabbed his dick and feasted. He felt a surge of power she must have sensed, and stopped. He caught his breath. She came up to him and gave him a playful kiss. The look on her face said… more… sex. His heart raced. She stretched herself out and pulled him on top. Now, it was him exploring her. Her skin was soft, delicate, and every touch increased his desire. Wave after wave of pleasure shot through him. Her strokes, their movement, this was better than anything…anything? Just like that, his mind did a 180. His thoughts no longer focused…wandered. What about the game tomorrow? Was he going to give that up for this? He slowed. A gnawing chill replaced the heat. Was this Chicago all over again? He turned away from her kiss.

"Something wrong?" she asked between gasps. Her eyelids fluttered open.

"No, no, nothing's wrong." What the hell could be wrong? She was every man's dream come to life. Perfect in every way.

"Then, you know, come on." She kissed him hard and reached for him. "Wait a minute, what happened? You didn't…"

He flipped off of her. "No, I didn't. It's just, well, I can't. I mean, I can, but I won't."

"What the fuck are you talking about? We're naked and we've touched everything there is to touch. What's the problem?"

He knew he couldn't explain. No, he didn't want too. Strange, fucking someone was considered the most intimate, but in reality it wasn't. It was what was behind the act, the person, and their lives, that was the intimacy, not fucking. "I think you should go," he said.

"What? I'm going to say we did it anyway. Might as well finish what we started."

"Say whatever, but we're done."

She slid up on the mattress and pulled the bed sheet around her. "I can't believe it. Pitchers. They really are strange, not like outfielders. They go for the glory. You get your kicks by teasing, promising a finish, and then puff, you're onto something else. You're batshit crazy. I hope the Yanks murder you. Sonofabitch. So close. Shit."

She scooted off the bed and dressed while he found his pants. She turned to him when they were by the door. "This is a first. I've never... I don't...you're a goddamn shit, bastard—"

He opened the door and gave her a slight nudge. "You'll get over it, honest," and watched her walk down the hall, not believing he had kicked her out. He listened, then double-locked the door. When he felt enough time had passed, he went slowly to a chair near the TV and fell in. He stared at the blank screen wondering what the fuck had happened. Was the whole Brown Derby thing a setup? Danny, Carlie, no Carrie, did they work for the mob? What about tomorrow? His team was a game away from becoming World Series champions. The sound of those words...

He let out a breath. He stood and paced. Danny warned him about girls like...Carrie. All she wanted was to fuck a major leaguer, do a World Series winning pitcher. He chewed that over. He was being paranoid, although he had good reason to be. He stopped near the floor to ceiling windows that over looked the highway and the mountains. Even at this hour of the night, the road was full of cars heading anywhere. It had to be coincidence. The girl only wanted a notch, a claim to fame. None of this had anything to do with the thug in the bathroom. He should have felt better, but didn't. He was alone in a suite that had a living room/

dining room combination and an endless master bedroom.

His father would never believe this luxury. He wouldn't have believed a lot of things. "No, that's not right," Jack said and went back to the chair. He plunked down into the seat. Nah, his father would have understood. His father would have enjoyed all this. And the thug? He would figure a way. He'd do what was necessary to survive. Jack gazed around the room. "Shit, shit, shit. Come on, Dad, what should I do? I need your magic." There was only silence.

His father knew him as no one else. "Brains," he'd say, "not so much, but you have a *gutah nashmah*, a good soul, and a hell of an arm."

Jack got up and went toward the window and looked out again. Tomorrow was the biggest day of his life. His teammates were counting on him. Should he throw it away? Should he run like the last time? He touched the bruises on his stomach. Apparently, Carrie never noticed. She must have been too into…who knew or cared? At least he sacrificed something for the team.

He grabbed a shirt from the couch and decided to go for a smoke. He went for his jacket. He needed to get out talk to someone. He sighed and rubbed his face. This was going nowhere. He stuck his hand in his coat pocket and felt a card. He studied it. It was Fred's. "*Aahh.*" He stuffed it back. He rocked on his feet. There was something about Fred. Maybe it was the Yiddish, a similar background. But he was a *reporter* who made a living in finding things. Shit, what if he learned about Chicago and the girl? His imagination took over. He put his jacket on and went to the door. His hand was on the knob. Hold it. What if they just talked? The most important game of the year was tomorrow. That was a conversation in and of itself. Damn, there was no one else. He held the card and stared at it. What the hell?

## Chapter Forty-Nine

# 2015 – Chicago

Billy Dee took McNulty's phone. He hesitated as to whom to call first. It was going to be messy either way. He walked out of the room for privacy and dialed his wife.

"Hello, Janine?"

She sounded as if she had been awake.

"Just called to let you know I've been caught up in police business. Don't want you to worry."

"I wasn't," she said. "I figure if there was something I'd get a call."

He looked at the phone.

"Everything okay with you?"

"Not a thing wrong. I've been doing some cleaning and cooking like I always do."

He swallowed and his hand got sweaty. Oh, Lord, something's going on. His wife didn't do those things. Not at this hour of the night. "Baby, I'll be home soon."

"Billy Dee, you be careful."

"Always." She hung up. He went back into the room and gave McNulty his phone.

"You all right?" McNulty asked.

Billy Dee strapped on his gun. "Huh?"

"I asked if everything was okay?"

He gave McNulty a look. "Yeah, sure. Hey, how much time passed since Majuski left here?"

McNulty looked at his watch. "I'd say, give or take, at least twenty-thirty minutes. Why?"

"I got a feeling he's no longer in the hospital."

Their gaze met.

"Where is he then?" McNulty asked.

"I gotta go."

"But, an officer is coming down to interview you."

"Can't wait," and he hurried out as best he could.

***

Billy Dee's tires squealed as he hit the gas and drove out of the parking lot. "Something ain't right." He went for his phone by instinct, then remembered it was gone. At least the bastard didn't get his gun. He flew down the city streets. There was little traffic. Why would Majuski be after him and his wife? Hell, the cocksucker left him for dead. Why mess with Janine? He tapped his hand on the wheel. He could feel his anger. He'd empty ten rounds into the motherfucker if his wife were harmed. Ain't goin' to be no talkin' or advising of fuckin' rights. No sir…point and shoot. Although it had been awhile since he'd used his piece. He was once a pretty good shot. Well, he was a hell of lot younger, but the eye never goes away. He'd know what to do. He looked at the clock on the dash. Ten minutes had gone by and in another ten he'd be home. He made a series of turns. He was in his neighborhood. There was the gas station, the coffee shop two blocks down, Pete's Pizza, and then his block. He made a left onto Drexel. His street was a mix of small apartment buildings and bungalows. He parked several building down from his. He killed the engine and the lights and prayed the goddamn door didn't squeak when he opened and closed it. He stayed in the shadows as best he could until he neared his house. The nightlights that were usually on were off. Should he go through the front, the back, or the basement door? He could hear himself breathe, and even though it was cool outside, he had to wipe the sweat off his face. He took a minute to gather himself. The basement was best. Unexpected. One thing for sure, he knew his way around even in the dark.

He walked along the side of the house. His hand touched the bricks for guidance. Near the middle of the building was a railing perpendicular to the side. He felt his way around the barrier to the three-step staircase that led to the basement door. He avoided the rake and shovel placed there on some forgotten Sunday and got his keys. The light reflected from the night sky helped him identify the right one. So far, so good. The lock had to be jiggled with just enough pressure. Twice he failed. He cussed and threatened that if he lived through this, he'd destroy the goddamn lock, and then added, "Please, Mary and Joseph, open."

It did. He stepped in. The light from the outside was limited. He was enveloped in darkness a few feet into the laundry room. He stepped carefully, but stumbled on something. "Damn," he hissed, and waited. Silence. The staircase leading to the kitchen was to his right through the room. He knew there was a flashlight on a shelf on the opposite wall. He walked like a blind man with his hands outstretched. It seemed to take forever to get to the other side. He touched the wall and used his hands to locate the light. Success. He took a deep breath and pointed the flashlight toward the floor. The batteries must have worn down; the light was dim. His wife wouldn't be happy. He could hear her scolding him. "I told you, Billy Dee, check those double D's. The electricity go out when there's a big storm." If he had been lookin' at her, he wouldn't be quite sure what she meant. It don't matter now. He prayed that she was still there to see. He looked down at the flashlight. "Give me enough juice to get to the staircase."

He crouched a bit and moved slowly. When he got to the first step, he put the light on the stair and unholstered his gun. At his age, he was going to use two hands, just like he was trained all those years ago. There were nine stairs between the basement and the kitchen. Each step creaked a little louder as he made his way. He took more time. As he neared the top, he looked up. Shit, the door. Usually, Janine left it open and unlocked. It was definitely shut. He moved to the side of the stair so his body would be at a 90-degree angle to the door. He shifted his weapon to his right and tried the knob with his left hand. As he turned it, he leaned his left shoulder into the frame. Locked. He wiped his face with his sleeve. Why the hell would his wife do that? He was breathing heavily again. He had to think. The door must be Majuski's work. The sonofabitch was thorough. He looked down the staircase at the flashlight resting on the bottom step. He looked at the door. Somewhere on his key ring was the one for this lock. He had no choice but to get the light.

He holstered the gun and went down the stairs. The flashlight flickered when he held it under his arm and shined it on the keys. "Come on, baby, don't die on me now." He went as quickly as he could as the beam dimmed into darkness. Shit. He at least succeeded to find two possibilities. He separated them from the ring and went up the stairs. This time there was no light. He counted the stairs so he wouldn't bang into the door. On the ninth step, he reached out and felt the wood barrier. He searched for the doorknob and then with one hand, felt his way a few inches above for the keyhole. The first key failed. Sonofabitch. Sweat trickled down his face. Okay, this got to be the one.

He jiggled the lock and called upon Jesus. The key didn't move. His frustration mounted. He touched his holster. He could shoot his way in. After a second or two, he gave up that idea. He tried the key again, but this time, while he played with the lock he pulled the handle toward him. The sweet sound of a click greeted him. Okay, I'm in.

He opened the door and took out his gun. There was a nightlight at the end of the kitchen and another in the bathroom next to it.

The rumble of the furnace, water dripping from some faucet, the creaking of a sleeping house, noises usually ignored or not even heard, greeted him with every step. He made it through the kitchen and edged up to the bathroom. The hallway that led to the front door had a staircase to the second floor on his right and the living room on his left. He crouched and held his breath. He peered through the slats of the staircase for a second and then swung his arms with the gun pointed into the living room.

"Janine?"

## Chapter Fifty

# Berlin – 1938

The guard shoved Pyotr into the cell, then slammed the door. "Wait, what happened? I want to speak with Herr Brach." His hands gripped the bars. "Officer."

"*Schweigen*, keep quiet." The guard turned away.

"Please," he said to the fading echo of the officer's boots.

Pyotr's hands slid down the bars as the rest of him collapsed to the floor. He squeezed his eyes and fought to keep his composure. "I am going to die here," he repeated to himself. A tear ran down his cheek.

"If you think like that, you might as well find a knife and end your pathetic life."

Pyotr used his sleeve to wipe his face. He stumbled to his feet. "What?"

Another prisoner had been sitting on a stool-like bench in a darken corner of the same cell. His shirtsleeves were torn. He seemed like it had been days since he shaved and even Pyotr could smell the man's unwashed body. His arms were like sticks and his hair flew in every direction.

"The name is Grossman, prisoner number J-10677. Like you, I am enjoying the same wonderful hospitality of the Third Reich. Heil Hitler."

Pyotr stayed by the bars. "Your German is not very good. Where are you from?"

"You want to know where I'm from? *Hmm.*" His stare pierced the distance. "A Jew is from everywhere and nowhere. We have no place. We have no land and no country wants us. We are a nation of *luftmenchen.* We are the people of the air."

He held up his thumb and forefinger and rubbed them together.

Pyotr took a step toward Grossman. "A lanzman?"

"You want to look at my *schvanz* to make sure? The national pastime of this piece of shit country is throwing Jews in jail. They keep track of it like a sport."

"Mr. Grossman," he looked around. "*Shh,* they may hear you."

Grossman got up from the stool with much effort and limped towards Pyotr. "Mister, whatever trial you have is already done. The verdict is in. If death is the sentence, don't give the bastards the satisfaction. Murdering you is not enough; they want your will, your spirit. If they succeed to take it, the Nazis don't have to kill you, you're already dead."

Pyotr heard the door between the courtroom and the jail section open. He left Grossman and hurriedly went to the front of the cell. "Herr Brach?" He stretched to be able to see the corridor. A male and female guard came into view. Between them was a woman and behind her a man he recognized as the prosecutor, Herr Schmidt.

"Step back from the bars," Schmidt ordered.

Pyotr didn't move.

"Are you deaf?"

The female officer took a wood baton from her belt and swung it at the front of the cell. Pyotr dodged the blow. They all laughed except the woman between the guards.

Schmidt turned to the woman. "Fraulein, this is the man who had sex with you." He said it more as a statement than a question.

The female guard nudged the woman forward.

"Look," Schmidt said, "this is the man, *jah*?"

Her eyes were wide. There were red bruises on her face. Her hair was long and uncombed. Schmidt put his hand around the back of the woman's neck. "We appreciate your talents accommodating our young gallant men. I am asking in the name of the Vaterland."

She turned her head slightly. "I fuck our soldiers because I have no choice, and when I become too grotesque you will dispose of me like you did Franz."

She let out a yelp. Schmidt must have pressed harder. "Listen, you fuckin' whore, while you still have the privilege to breathe, this is the man."

Pyotr saw her mouth move, but there was no sound. Schmidt held onto her and motioned for the guards to enter the cell. "Maybe you'll only recognize him by his dick."

"I've seen many," she said.

"I'm sure that's true, but how many were circumcised?"

The guards grabbed Pyotr. The female guard attacked his pants.

"Stop," she said, "okay, this is the man."

"He forced himself on you?" Schmidt asked.

"*Jah,*" and then quietly added, "just like the others."

Pyotr was left standing in the middle of the cell. He held the top of his pants tightly. "What hell is this?" He turned to where his cellmate sat. Grossman had his head back resting on the wall and mouth open. Pyotr went to him.

"Grossman, are you sleeping? How can you sleep? Did you see what they did? I never touched that girl. Are you listening?" He waited a few seconds. The man was still. He looked to see if he was breathing. "Grossman?" He grabbed his hand. It was cold. He pressed his fingers on Grossman's wrist. There was no pulse. "My God." He took a deep breath and stared at the body. "He's dead."

A chill went through him. He rubbed his arms and moved

a few steps away. He should have tears. A man died. Instead, he surprised himself. A smile crept over his face. The sonofabitch cheated the bastards. He died on his own terms. He stood over Grossman and recited the ancient prayer and reaffirmation of faith from centuries past. "Shema Yisrael, Hear Oh Israel, the Lord our God the Lord is one."

## Chapter Fifty-One

# Los Angeles – 1981

Jack dialed Fred's number. The phone rang several times before he answered. His voice was groggy. "Hello, who the hell is this?"

"It's Jack Rakow. You sound like you've been sleeping."

"What the hell do you think I was doing? What time is it anyway?"

"I'm not wearing a watch. I don't know."

"Jesus. It's still dark outside, isn't it? Don't you have to rest for tomorrow's game?"

"Yeah, you're right. I thought if…"

"I'm too old to party all night and then function well the next day."

"I understand. Sorry to bother you."

Neither spoke. After several seconds, Fred said, "Okay, you got me up. What's on your mind, *boychik*?"

"Nothing."

"Nothing? You call me in the middle of the night about nothing? Think, Jack, what's going on in that noggin of yours?"

"No really, this was a bad idea. I'm sorry."

"You sound terrible, and I know it's not from sleeping. It's only one baseball game, Jack. I promise you no matter what we reporters write, the sun will rise the day after."

"Good to know." He paused.

"*Boychik*, you sound worse than me. I have no idea what fuckin' time it is but I'll meet you at the bar in your hotel… say, twenty minutes. Make sure your manager doesn't catch you. *Farshteyn*, understand?"

" Sure. Thanks."

***

The hotel lounge was nearly empty. Three women and a few guys sat around the large U-shaped bar. It seemed they were each other's last call.

"What can I get you?" the bartender asked.

"Johnny Black on the rocks." Jack stood and waited for his drink.

"There are plenty of seats."

"Thanks, I'll find a table in the back. I'm expecting another person."

The bartender gave him a wry smile. "Hey, more power to you."

One of the women erupted with a sharp laugh after a man said something.

Jack took his drink and went to the farthest table from the bar. He wore sunglasses and sat facing away from the entry-way. He gulped down the first drink. The scotch warmed him. He turned in his seat to see if Fred had arrived. He noticed the woman with the laugh had moved closer to one of the guys. No Fred. He picked up his empty glass and sucked the melted ice. Fred should have been here by now. *This was a bad idea. He isn't coming.* Jack drummed his fingers on the table. After another minute, he ordered a second. The bartender brought the drink. He stared, admiring the amber color of the scotch. *The hell with Fred.* He wrapped his hand around the glass.

"Whoa. Jesus, what the…? God, it's…you scared the crap out of me."

Fred took his hand off Jack's shoulder. "Obviously you never read about Marshal Wild Bill Hickok, *boychik*. Never have your back to the door."

"Thanks, I'll read up on him." Jack grabbed a napkin to wipe the spilled liquid off his sleeve.

"You started without me. How many have you had?"

"Only two, but most of the second is on my hand and table."

Fred took a seat across from him. "Sorry about that. What's with the shades? Too bright down here in the middle of the night?"

"No, I thought, well… I didn't want to be seen."

Fred looked at him. "You're even more fucked up than you were on the phone. Take those damn things off. You're not Clark Kent."

He took the glasses off and dropped them on the table.

"So what's up, *bubbeleh*?" Fred asked while he waived his hand to get the bartender's attention.

Jack felt like the count was three and two and the bases were loaded. He had to come in with a strike. What bullshit can he throw that won't be stupid? "I think we're going to win it in six. I've got a good feeling."

Fred gave him a funny look interrupted by the drinks the bartender delivered. "That's a headline," he said.

"No really. We've got a great team."

"Uh-huh, so do the Yanks."

Jack sipped his drink. "Yeah I guess. I don't know. We're so close. My dad warned me when I was a kid not to get ahead of myself."

"Yeah? Tell me about your dad."

## Chapter Fifty-Two

# Berlin – 1938

"Guard. Guard!" Pyotr yelled, clutching the cell bars. His shouts were ignored. It didn't surprise him. He was becoming numb to the unending brutality of the Nazis. In the months awaiting charges, the nightly beatings and screams were his bedtime music. Fear was their currency. Humanity had gone to hell. He went to the back of the cell and sat next to Grossman. "Which one of us is better off?" He studied the dead man's face. Who was he? He never asked Grossman why he was there. What crime did he commit? Pyotr stopped himself... Other than being a Jew. He sighed.

"Grossman, maybe you have something in your pocket. A cigarette?" He was about to reach in, but stopped. What if the bastards saw him go through them? He walked to the front of his cell and looked down the corridor. It was clear. The Nazis were most likely enjoying their *hasenpfeffer* for lunch. When was the last time he ate? He didn't remember. The food wasn't worth remembering...stale bread and a bowl of something that resembled soup.

He sidled back to Grossman. He dug his hands into Grossman's front pants pockets—not even a crumb. He stared at the body. He noticed Grossman's hands. They weren't on his lap, but dangled—one in front of him and the other near the wall.

"Grossman your face, you're hiding something." He reached behind and felt a packet in between the wall and the bench. He wrestled it from its hiding place and went to another dark corner and opened his palm. He held a bundle of Reichsmarks in 50s and 100s. He was about to count it when he heard a door open.

Shit. He thrust his hand into his pocket, but realized that was stupid. He undid his pants and put the bundle in his underwear. He zipped up quickly and ran to the front. "Help, help, a man is dead."

A guard he hadn't seen before approached the cell.

"What did you say?"

"I said, there's a dead man in the corner."

"A Jew…dead in the corner?" he asked.

The news didn't seem to have an effect. The guard shined his flashlight. "*Hmm*," he grunted. "What is his number?

Pyotr's mouth went dry. "His number?"

The guard directed his question to the corpse. "Your number? *Was sind sie?* What are you called?"

There was no response.

"Excuse me," Pyotr said and pointed to Grossman, "he is dead and cannot answer."

The guard grabbed Pyotr through the bars and rammed his forehead on the steel. "We'll clean up the mess after we are done with you."

***

Pyotr was led out of the cell and marched into the courtroom. The guard pushed him into a cage. The front of it had a door with steel mesh. Inside was a small chair.

"Sit," the guard ordered, then slammed the door.

A few minutes later, Herr Brach came to the cage carrying an armload of papers.

"Herr Brach," Pyotr said as he rushed to the door.

His lawyer held up his hand. "Don't talk, listen. You've been charged with *rassenschande*. The Government accuses you of having sexual relations with Freida Weber at the Kabarett Musikspaß."

"What?"

"Quiet. The punishment is imprisonment or death. The prosecutor, Herr Schmidt, has advised me that their witness identified you and there are witnesses to the identification."

"But, she—"

Brach put on his reading glasses and read from a paper. "She told Herr Schmidt there was no doubt in her mind, it was you. She remembers because the night it happened the Kabarett burned down. She managed somehow to escape from your grasp after you had forced her to submit." He pointed to her signature at the bottom of the page.

He took off his glasses and turned to Pyotr. "Do you have something to say?"

He took a breath. "For God's sake, Herr Brach, this is all made up. None of it is true. Believe me."

His lawyer's eyes twinkled and his lips formed a half smile. "I thought Jews were smart. Apparently, you must be one of the few who are dumb. What is your evidence? Your word? The word of a Hebrew?" He shook his head. "In the Reich's eyes you are guilty. They don't have to prove it. You have to show your innocence. If you force this case to trial you will be signing your death warrant. Your life is in your hands."

*Chapter Fifty-Three*

# Los Angeles – 1981

Jack finished his drink and ordered another. He played for time as he slid the empty glass back and forth between his hands. "You want to know about my dad?"

"Sure, it's a good place as any."

"What's to tell? He survived the war."

Fred put his hand on Jack's. "Hold on, *boychik*, surviving the war wasn't like striking out a minor leaguer. It's an accomplishment. He beat the bastards. My adopted mother told me my real father went to Germany before the war and didn't come back."

Jack met his gaze. "Why did he do that?"

Fred shrugged. "I have no answer. I think I became a reporter because I'm searching. I've spent a lot of time trying to find who my real parents were. Names change and memories disappear. It's difficult to get survivors to talk about that time in their lives."

Jack grasped his empty glass. It still felt cold. "Here's the thing," he spoke to the glass. "When your parent are survivors, there is a separation between you and everyone else. It wasn't because of the accents and broken English, although that didn't help. It was the way they went about everyday living that singled us out. My mother's greeting whether answering the phone or in person was 'What's wrong? Are you all right?' That fear or anxiety was baked into me. Do you know what it's like to be afraid, every day?"

He looked straight at Fred. "My father, jeez, if there was an easy way to do something like a straight line between two points, he'd find the most difficult route. Do you get what I'm saying?"

Fred nodded. "Amen to that. There was always fear that something bad was about to happen. Where was your dad from?"

The bartender brought Jack's third scotch. He pointed at Fred and told him to freshen his drink. "You got to keep up," Jack said when Fred protested. "You want to ask questions… drink."

"I'll keep up, I'm from good Polish stock. Vodka is like mother's milk. *Na zdrowie!* Cheers."

"My father was from Warsaw. We'll be able to drink till morning." Jack struck the table with his fist.

"I'm sure we could, but come game time I hit a typewriter, and you'll have to throw a baseball for strikes."

"Good point, but as you said, it's only one game." He burst into laughter. "One game, my ass. It's what this whole damn thing is about."

Fred took a sip of his drink. "What are you talking about?"

"Jesus, Fred, follow the ball. All players tell reporters how meaningful a game is. If they don't, management comes down on them, or they're labeled 'bad attitude.' But when that umpire shouts 'play ball,' it won't matter how many scotches I had, I know what it means."

Jack bumped the table as he tried to get up.

"Where are you going?"

"What? Nowhere, just making a point." He sat down and reached for his drink. "My father survived the *arbeit* camps and Dachau—somehow. Seven years, can you imagine? Seven fuckin' years of death and starvation, but he did it. The US army found him at Dachau and thought he was a corpse lying in the dirt. A soldier heard a faint hum. The son of a gun was humming Chopin. He was a music professor before the war. It's goddamn hard to believe. The Army doctors brought him back to life. As crazy as that is, he met my mother there—Katalyna."

"No shit."

"I've got a picture." He reached into his pocket and struggled to pull out his wallet. "Hold on. Damn pants, everything has to fit tight. Here." The picture was in between a faded and worn 50 Reichsmark.

"What's this?" Fred asked and pointed to the German money.

"Oh. That? It was a gift from my dad. He told me to hold onto it for luck. When he was taken to one of the many work camps, he managed to hide some money. I don't know how he did it or where the Reichsmarks came from. But it saved his life until Dachau. Then thank God, time ran out on the Nazi bastards."

"Hell, Jack, this isn't a story, it's a book, a movie. Can I touch it?"

"Sure."

Fred reached for the money and picture.

"Barkeep, another round," Jack said and pointed to the table.

Fred looked up. "Okay, last one." He looked at the picture. "When was this taken?"

"1945 or '46. They were living in Munich."

"Look at your mother in that Chanel-like hat. She was a beauty, and your dad. Wow. How old was he? His hair is all gray."

"I think late twenties or early thirties."

"Huh. They look happy, like the war never happened."

Jack leaned forward and studied the picture. "Yeah, I guess

so, at least from the outside. My mother never forgot. My father told me before the war she had been some sort of courier. She took unbelievable risks. But the war took the best out of her. She never forgot her suffering and fear. My father allowed himself to get on with life."

Fred picked up his freshened drink. "To your parents and survival."

"To Mom and Dad." Jack clinked his glass and held it in the air.

"Is there more?" Fred asked.

"More what?"

"Did you want to add something to the toast?"

"Yeah, I do."

"Well?"

His hand shook slightly. "When I get into the game, Fred, no matter what, I'm going to kill the Yankees." He threw his head back and swallowed his drink.

# Chapter Fifty-Four

# 2015 – Chicago

Billy Dee's wife had duct tape across her mouth and was tied to the couch.

"Janine, baby, are you okay?" Billy Dee lowered his gun and went to her.

She made a muffled noise that stopped him. Was Majuski still in the house? He went into a crouch and clutched his gun with both hands. "Come on out, you bastard."

He raised his voice. He went room to room. There was no sign of him. He went back to his wife. "Baby, he's gone. Billy Dee is here and will take care of you."

He came toward her and again she made a soft noise. He looked closer and realized what appeared to be ropes were wires that went from his wife's neck down her shoulders to behind the couch.

He went to the end of the sofa and got on his hands and knees. He saw a cylinder dangling and more wires that ran to a box. Holy shit, his wife was attached to a bomb. Lord have mercy. He stood up. "Baby, I don't know how, but it's going to be all right. Don't move. I'm going to hit the lights. I need to have a better look. If Majuski is still here, having light won't matter. The explosive will blow all of us to hell."

He flicked the switch and froze. He looked around the room. Nothing blew up. He moved slowly to his wife and dabbed the perspiration from her face. She sat very still. "I know you're scared, baby. I'm going to take a look." Her eyes twitched. "Take deep breaths," he said, "concentrate on the breathing."

If she only knew he had no idea what to do. He was making it up as he went along. He gave her a quick glance, then leaned over the back of the couch and peered into the space. The red cylinder was suspended by wires and hung midway to the floor. He studied the object. Chinese writing appeared on the side. He was stunned. Could it be?

"Holy fuckin' shit." His laugh began slow and grew. His hand was about to pound the back of the sofa but his wife's high-pitched sound stopped him.

"You're okay," he said and went to her. He gently took the wire collar from her neck and laid it on one of the cushions. Her gaze was like beams of light ready to explode.

"I'm going to take the tape off. I'll do it quickly, but it may hurt. Here it goes." She yelped when the tape came off, and then fell into his arms.

"He was going to kill me. Why were you laughing?" she said in between sobs. Her hands balled into fists. "What's wrong with you? He told me you were dead. Billy Dee. I was so scared I couldn't move." She wrapped her arms around her body to stop from shaking. "I'm so cold."

"No one's going to hurt you, Janine, not while I'm around." He held her until she calmed. "Let me get you a drink. We all can use one.

He went into the kitchen and found a bottle of bourbon. "You ain't going to believe it, Janine, but you weren't hooked up to an explosive." He brought her a glass.

"What? I don't understand."

"Drink some of that. It will do you good." He watched her take a couple of sips.

"That cylinder is some kind of Chinese firework."

She looked up. "No!"

He shook his head. "Sure is. The sonofabitch didn't want you to call the police. He wanted to buy time. If I hadn't come along, oh dear Jesus, you would have sat there forever."

She burst into tears again. "This is a nightmare. Who? Why? What does all of this have to do with you…us?"

He took a deep breath. "Janine, I stumbled into one hell of a mess. I'm so sorry." He took her hand. "Tell me what happened. How did Majuski get in? What did he say?"

"He rang the doorbell and held up a badge. I thought… well, who knows…something happened to you. I let him in. We started talkin'. He asked if I knew… Billy Dee, I don't… wait, it was a woman's name."

"Melissa? Did he say Melissa Stone?"

She put her head between her arms. "I'm sorry, I… who is that?"

"It's okay, baby. Don't you worry." He gathered her in his arms and gently patted her back. He stared into space and silently thanked God for their lives.

She lifted her head from his shoulder. "Billy Dee, whatever happened to that prisoner who went missing?"

"Prisoner?" His mind came back. "Jack Rakow."

"I think that's the name. He was a baseball player?"

He stared at his wife. " Rakow, Jesus, that's it."

"What's it?" she asked.

"Jack Rakow. Are you okay?" He got to his feet.

"Yes, I think my heart is back to first gear. What is your little head up to?"

"Lock the doors and don't let anyone in unless it's me."

"Billy Dee, after all we've been through?"

"I know," he let out a sigh, "but I'm in too deep to let go. I'm going to surprise one mother…"

## Chapter Fifty-Five

# New York -1981

Jack kicked dirt off the pitching rubber. The scoreboard showed his name and number as the Dodgers pitcher. They were ahead and if he did his job, they would win the World Series. The catcher flashed the signs calling for pitches. No use playing around. It was like an outside force powered his arm. If that was because his father looked down, Jack silently thanked him. He would just throw what he wanted. The hitters, like his catcher, never knew what was coming.

The first batter struck out. The catcher held the ball after the third strike and shouted at Jack. He threw to the second hitter and the pitch went by the backstop. His catcher got up from his crouch. "What'cha doing?"

Jack smiled. On the next pitch, the second hitter hit a fly ball for an out. The third Yankee batter watched two balls sail past him and the catcher. Time was called. The catcher sprinted to the mound. Jack knew his battery mate was upset.

"What the hell are you doing, Jack?"

"I'm pitching."

"For God's sake, look at the signs."

"Hey, there's only two kinds of pitches in me today—fastball or curve. That's what I'm throwing. I've got it. Just go back and catch."

He saw the catcher look into the dugout. Tommy Lasorda shrugged.

Jack was never better. The other night's threats were pushed away for another time. All he saw was the catcher's target. He dug within himself and pitched to win.

\*\*\*

For the few hours after the game, he and his fellow LA Dodgers were champions. His teammates poured Champagne over his head, and he soaked it all in. He was for a moment part of something great. They partied on the flight home and at their hotel. As the celebration broke up, in the early morning hours, he spotted Fred and invited him up for a nightcap. They were feeling no pain and their voices were loud as they walked down the hotel corridor to Jack's room.

"*Shh*," Fred said, "You'll wake everyone up."

Jack screwed up his face. "Oh, sorry," he said softly. "I'm going to Disneyland, everybody," he shouted.

"Jack!"

"Okay, I'll tone it down. Holy shit, we're at my place already?" Jack stood in front of the door.

"What are you waiting for?" Fred asked.

Jack turned. "Ah, my key."

They burst out laughing.

"Try your pocket, dumb ass."

"Oh, yeah." Jack stuck the key in the lock and pushed. He stepped inside. Something caught his eye and he looked down. A scrap of paper lay on the threshold. He scooped it up.

"You are a dead man. Murderer."

Fred had wandered into the hallway and made his way into the room. "*Boychik*, the ladies are slipping you notes?"

Jack blushed and stuffed the paper in his pocket. He felt

his stomach churn. Shit. "Well… I am champion of the world." He looked away for a second and then forced a smile.

"W-o-m-e-n." Jack drew out the word. After a pause, he asked, "Are you married? Do you have kids?" He opened the liquor cabinet and searched for a bottle of vodka.

"The ball player turns into a reporter. How do you like that? Well, I am married and I have a daughter. She is eleven months old."

Jack gave him his drink. "A daughter? Fatherhood? What's that like?"

Fred's face turned serious. "It's like what you did today, even better. This was a game. Children are real. They are what's left after you are gone. It's a challenge to do it right."

"Wow, h-e-a-v-y at three or is it four in the morning."

"You asked."

"Yes I did." He lowered his glass. "It must have been tough for you."

"How so?"

"I mean, well, you didn't know who were your real parents."

Fred swallowed his drink. "I know I can hold my liquor."

Jack held up the bottle. "We're doing real good."

Fred was all business. "Here's what I pieced together." He waved his arm and let go of his glass. It bounced on the carpet. "When the war broke out my father still hadn't returned from Germany. Within two years, the Nazis took over Warsaw and well, things went from bad to worse for the Jews. I was told life was so horrible my mother gave me to a Polish woman who knew my father from some university."

"Your father went to a university?"

Fred shrugged. "I'm telling you what I know, *putz*."

"Sorry, go on."

"She in turn had a friend in Łódź. That's how bad it was. War turned many into monsters as well as heroes. I was lucky and thankful every day."

Jack refilled the glasses. "You're one hell of a sonofabitch."

"Not nearly as tough and prickly as our folks."

"I'll drink to that."

They emptied the bottle. By the time the sun rose, Fred left the hotel and Jack wasn't far behind. He went out the back. The buzz from the liquor hadn't lessened his worry. The note was still in his pocket. He searched the street before he stepped out and caught a cab. He was condemned to live in fear, never knowing when the bastards would strike.

***

Fear claimed Jack. Fear as if he was reliving his parents' stories of survival from the Nazis. YOU ARE A DEAD MAN played in his head. This time, it wouldn't be the sound of marching jackboots. It could be the guy on the corner or the woman at the bar who had the seductive smile. It was the Ambassador West and Linzie's murder all over again. As Jack rode in the cab, a recitation from the Jewish High Holidays popped into his head. It was a prayer that listed the good and bad that may happen in the year to come. Who by fire, who by drowning… He put his hands over his face. He hadn't thought of the High Holidays for years. Was he about to be punished for his nonobservance? *Holy shit.* He stared out the window. Now anyone could be the one to end his life. He had to get away.

Jack never pitched again. If the Dodgers had called, he wouldn't have known. He didn't answer his phone or check his mail. He left town. He stayed at out-of-the-way motels for no more than forty-eight hours. They weren't the accommodations he had grown accustomed to as a major league ball player. The bed sheets were thin, as well as the walls. Johnny Walker helped him get through the nights. Sometimes when he went for ice, he bumped into the floozy who occupied the next room. Even in his drunken state, he had standards. In the afternoon, he'd drive down I-40 toward Arizona. The car was old and rusted in the front. The air conditioner didn't work. He would sweat through his shirts. Some nights, instead of going to his room, he would find the nearest dive until closing. The women at those joints wore jeans that looked two sizes too small and they spilled out of them. Their faces showed that the years hadn't been kind. They knew all the pick-up lines a man had and could drink most of them under the table. He spent a small fortune on whiskey and cigarettes. He woke every morning in a stupor and coughed his lungs out.

A month passed. "Who shall *fuckin'* live. And who shall *fuckin'* die. Who by fire and who by water…" The prayer still haunted him.

He stopped reading road signs. He didn't know where he was or care. Arizona? Nevada? It didn't matter.

He had pulled off the highway late one night and checked in at the first place off the road. In the morning, from his room he saw a phone booth near the entrance of the motel. He stumbled toward it. He had the receiver in his hand and a fistful of change. Who to call? Danny the Dodger PR guy? He put the change down and fumbled for his wallet. A card with the name Brown Derby fell out. "Shit." He bent to pick it up. Hey he could give that waitress… He rubbed his face to remember… Carrie, that's it. She had come to his room the night before the game. "What a piece of ass. J-e-s-u-s." Her naked image flashed across his mind and was gone just as quick.

An 18-wheeler passed while he had the phone in his hand and blew a gust of wind. He used his sleeve to wipe the dirt from his eyes. His gaze followed the disappearing truck. "Shit, that ain't going to happen. Oh hell." He put a dime in the slot and heard the dial tone. He'd call Fred.

Fred would know what to do. He put in more change and began to dial. But before the connection was made he hung up. *What the fuck could I say? Fred, a woman was killed back in Chicago some years ago, and the mob has been after me since.* No, this was his problem, his alone. He walked back to the motel room. He sat on the creaky bed and stared into the small mirror above the plastic wood-like bureau. There was some scotch left in the bottle and he reached for it. He took a swig and spit it out.

"I can't sit around waiting," he said. "No more." The bottle slipped from his hand. The bastards couldn't get him if he disappeared.

## Chapter Fifty-Six

# Japan - 1983

Jack stood in line at the airport. The way he figured, Japan was thousands of miles from the US and while he hated the food, he did have a good run playing ball. The Japanese called him *maitiamu*—mighty arm. Well he would play under that name... *Jacko Maitiamu*.

he Japanese, however, did not tolerate drunks. The honky-tonks hadn't moved from the last time he was there, but he didn't go. He even cut down on smoking. He still knew some agents. After a month in Tokyo, he looked one up. American players called him Jimmy, *Chikako*, in Japanese. Jack found Jimmy's number and convinced him to have lunch.

Jack walked into the restaurant wearing a beige sport jacket and sunglasses. His hair was combed and he looked and felt much better. The hostess led him to Jimmy's table where a bottle of sake stood at the ready. Jimmy got up and made a slight bow as did Jack.

"*Hisashiburi,* long time no see," Jimmy said.

Jack smiled. "I got lucky in LA."

They sat and Jimmy poured. "To your World Series victory." They clinked glasses.

A young woman with long dark hair brought a plate of sushi. Jack's gaze lingered on her and he only heard Jimmy say, "try...very good."

The woman stood near him ready to serve.

"*Arigato gozaimasu,* thank you," Jack said. She dropped a few pieces on his plate. *More goddamn raw fish. What I would give for a Big Mac. How am I going to live in this place?* He smiled at her when she asked if they needed anything else.

Japanese culture, unlike American, was indirect. They chatted about everything but the reason why they were having lunch. Jack managed to eat what was served and washed it down with a lot of sake. Near the end of the meal, the same waitress appeared. She and Jimmy spoke rapidly in Japanese. She bowed, turned, and left. Jack thought he saw a hint of a smile.

"What was that about?" Jack asked.

"She is pretty, yes?"

Jack leaned in his chair. "Yes, very."

"She liked you. She was excited when I told her you were an American baseball player."

"Yeah?" He wondered where this was going.

"Americans, as you know, do well here. The people think you are gods. So *maitiamu,* you have come back to play in Japan?

"Not exactly. I want to coach."

"Coach, why? I watched you pitch."

"Those days are over. The sixth game of the World Series was my last."

Jimmy drank his sake and shook his head. After a few minutes' pause, he said, "I'll see what I can do."

They stood and bowed. "Tell me where you're staying," Jimmy said. "Your American charm still works well with the ladies." Amusement flashed on his face as he nodded toward the other tables where the waitress was serving.

\*\*\*

Jack was alone in his hotel room. Jimmy had called a few days after the lunch and told him the Yomiuri Giants of Tokyo were interested. The rest of the conversation faded after Jimmy slipped in that the girl wanted to meet him. Tonight was the night.

## Chapter Fifty-Seven

# Tokyo- 1983

Jack became the pitching coach for the Yomiuri Giants. He didn't talk to the press and stayed in the bullpen before the game. He taught his pitchers some new tricks, and the team began to win.

He was enjoying Japan. Whenever the team played at home, at least, he now had someone. Whether it was after a night game or on an off day, all he needed to do was call and Aiko, the girl from the restaurant, would appear. He should have questioned it, but that was what sex does. He had heaven whenever he wanted and she was heaven. Jimmy was right. She thought him a god. Besides, he assured himself, he was thousands of miles from L.A.

The Giants were fighting for a playoff spot. They were a game behind and if they won their next one, the team would have a slot. Aiko came to his hotel room that night. They lay in bed, spent. Jack grabbed a cigarette. She curled up in his arms.

"Tomorrow is big game," she said.

"Yeah, it is. We should win. We'll have Egara pitching. He's been our best."

She nuzzled her face against his arm. "You sure? Egara has pitched a lot. Maybe Gotomara should start. He is just as good."

He pulled her to him. "Really? Since when do you follow this?"

She kissed him and reached between his legs. "I follow a lot."

There was no more conversation.

*** 

Gotomara got the nod after Jack discussed it with the manager, who didn't argue. He watched his pitcher throw. By the fourth inning, Gotomara's fastball didn't seem as fast and his curve didn't break. The opposing team hit him hard and the Giants lost the game. When he returned to his hotel room, the door was not locked. Thank God, Aiko must be waiting to cheer him up.

"Aiko? You there?" He stepped in. Was she in the bedroom…bathroom? The bathroom door was open but no Aiko. He went to the bedroom. On the bed was a pile of money. He felt his heart race. He checked the room, then flung the closet door open. No one was hiding behind his clothes. *What is going on?* After a few seconds, he moved closer to the bed. There were two thick stacks of hundred dollar bills. *Oh Jesus.* He grabbed the phone and called Aiko. The line was disconnected. He searched the room again. A piece of paper peeked out from under the money. He snatched it. "You very good coach. Ha Ha."

He'd call Jimmy, but then put the phone down. He got the picture. It was a setup from the beginning. He slumped into a chair. Jimmy must have known. During the time he was here, he had convinced himself he couldn't be found and didn't concern himself with shadows. But now… That stinkin' money was all "they" needed to force him to do whatever "they" wanted. Japan was no longer safe. He packed his clothes and left. The cash remained untouched.

He flew from Japan to Bangkok. He was still young enough to enjoy its pleasures, but wise enough to know "the pleasures" wouldn't last.

He became baseball's General MacArthur, island hopping across the Pacific until he came to Hawaii and settled in Maui in 2008. The sunsets were stunning, and every day was perfect. This could be the place he'd call home.

He had learned over the years to be meticulous with his belongings. Shirts were stacked in a color scheme. Underwear went into the third drawer, T-shirts in front. A picture of his parents sat on the nightstand near the bed. And he left a small piece of paper between the outside edge of the door and the jamb before leaving. He trained himself to notice detail. Shadows only gave him one chance.

He loosened up. He'd get the *LA Times* in the morning and read Fred's column. He became a hell of a tennis player and water-skied a few days a week. At night, he managed a bar. He even sent Fred a postcard to say hello and congratulate him on thirty years with the *Times*.

Three months later, he returned to his apartment and noticed the little paper in the door was gone. He didn't try the knob. He stood there for a few seconds staring at the spot where the paper had been. Then he took a breath and turned around. He walked a few blocks, looking over his shoulder.

He was done with island hopping, but what was next? Germany and Eastern Europe were out, even though the War ended sixty years ago. The stories of his parents' survival in those countries haunted him. London might be logical, but the bastards would also look there. Screw them.

He went to Paris. He became a physical trainer and soon had his own gym.

For all the beauty of the city, ghosts of the Second World War were present. Any street in Paris still had the scars of

Nazi occupation. The Hotel Lutetia had been the head-quarters of German military intelligence. The Gestapo had occupied 84 Avenue Foch. Despite the gaieties and bustle of the cafés, shadows of a different kind were all around.

Jack grew tired of all of it, the wine, the petite baguette, and even French women. There were no baseball games to listen to. The sports pages never had any news he cared about. He liked picking up the *LA Times* when he could get it and read Fred's column. It was his connection to home.

## Chapter Fifty-Eight

# 2014 - Chicago

Jack stopped at a café on the way to his gym. The news-paper stand on Avenue Victor Hugo had a copy of the *LA Times*. In Paris, there was always time for a café and a brioche. He took his seat and watched Parisians stroll by. He waited to open the paper until the waiter brought his coffee. He turned to the sports section.

There was a black banner across the top of Fred's column. In bold print, it said Fred had died and in place of his column was a still picture of him with a pad of paper talking to Tommy Lasorda, the former Dodgers manager. Jack put his cup down. Although Fred never knew, he had kept Jack going. His writing connected Jack to what his life had been. He stared into space. Time had rushed by him. Was it a lifetime since he heard his father's voice? Or in the hotel after the Series win that Fred told him how he survived the War?

His eyes became watery. It had been a long time since he'd felt the urge to cry. When he recovered, he paid the bill and took a walk. He went by buildings with signs in French, heard French spoken on the street. It all seemed so foreign, even though he had lived there for years. It was time to go home. Shadows remain shadows only until there is light. He needed to return to the US to pay his respects... whatever the danger.

He flew to LA and arrived ten minutes early for the funeral. Inside the chapel, people were in line to sign the registry. When it was his turn, he wrote his name but left no address. He took a program, found a seat in the back of the room. He glanced at the booklet. There were four speakers: the rabbi, of course, two colleagues, then Fred's daughter.

She looked like her old man. She was of the same height and had his wispy build. Her blonde hair was shoulder length, and she had Fred's smile. She walked to the podium, her eyes teary but resolute.

"My father," she began, "was a baseball fan through and through. Although his life began in Poland with a couple of strikes against him, he never let that get the better of him. He kept his eye on the ball and hit for average. His daily column was more than just a recitation of the game. He got into the players. He had the ability to get people to talk, and he wrote from their point of view. He looked at life as a baseball season with all its ups and downs: the comebacks, the victories and defeats. The game had to be played every day. That's how he lived. The beauty of baseball was the drama produced by the length of the season. You had to wait until the end of October to see how it turned out. Dad took each day as a gift. That joy was in his writing, and the conversations he had. It didn't matter who you were; he sought out your story. That was my Dad."

When the service ended, Jack introduced himself.

"I'm an old friend of your father. He was…" Jack held onto her hand. His eyes misted. "A *mensch*."

"Thank you." She slid her hand from his grip. "How did you know him?"

He did a quick look around the room and then in almost a whisper said, "I'm Jack Rakow. I pitched for the Dodgers in the 1981 World Series."

\*\*\*

It had been thirty-three years since that game. Jack grew to believe that the thugs who messed up his life were either dead, too old to care, or in jail. He moved to Chicago. To his surprise, sports people remembered him. ESPN did a story about Game 6 of the '81 Series. After that, he got a call from Fred's daughter. She had picked up from her father. They talked. She was the female version, complete with her use of the term 'boychik.' He promised to sit for an interview. But it didn't happen.

He became a regular at O'Brian's, the neighborhood bar, and became acquainted with Bobby Stegert, the athletic director at Lakeview High School. On a whim, he convinced Bobby to let him do some coaching. He had a blast. A photo of him appeared in the sports news in connection with that year's World Series.

A year went by. He stopped looking over his shoulder. He was home.

# Chapter Fifty-Nine

# 2015 – Chicago

To those who had bet on Jack and lost, the amount of time that passed was irrelevant. His debt had to be paid. It was only a question of when.

The last pitch of the 2015 World Series crowned a new team champion. In Chicago, someone whispered certain words to the right people, and the legal process that was dormant all those years woke from its slumber. The authorities learned of a suspect in the 1975 murder of Linzie Stevens at the Ambassador West Hotel.

***

It was Thursday morning. Jack was in his kitchen. He had just made a pot of coffee. There was a knock at the door. He looked out the window and saw a police car parked on the street. Two officers were on his front stoop. What the hell did they want? He turned the lock and opened the door.

"Good morning, fellows" he said with a smile. "What can I do for you?"

They had a grim look. "Are you Jack Rakow?" the officer with a mustache asked.

"Yeah, why?"

"You need to come with us."

"What's the problem?"

"We can discuss it at the station."

"I don't understand."

"Sir, don't make it more difficult."

He moved back from the door. The officers stepped in.

"Can I get a coat?"

The mustachioed officer answered. "Show me where and I'll get it."

Jack pointed to the front closet. "The black one."

He put the jacket on after the other officer patted him down. "Sorry, but we have to do this," he said, "I'll cuff you in front and not the back."

"I'm being arrested?"

"Yeah, I guess you are."

"For what?"

"We have a warrant for you. The charge is murder."

\*\*\*

He said he was FBI and called himself Lou George. O.B., who took Billy Dee's place at night, was the lock-up keeper at the police station at Belmont and Western. Billy Dee had told him before he left that evening about Jack Rakow and that he was to keep an eye on him.

"Don't want nothin' to happen while he's at the old 19th District," Billy Dee warned.

Now O.B. scratched his head when George handed over his government IDs. He looked at them from all angles in the light. They looked real. Besides, they were the Feds, and O.B. didn't want nothin' to do with them.

"Why is the Bureau interested in a retired baseball player?" He asked.

George drew himself up to his full five feet nine inches. "I'm just the delivery boy. Downtown wants him, not just for the murder, but interstate betting on major league games."

"Another Pete Rose?"

George shrugged. "They're all Shoeless Joe Jackson trying to make a buck."

"No problem, he's all yours. Just sign your 'John Hancock' and your FBI number."

He studied the signature, shrugged and got the prisoner.

"Thanks," George said, and gave Jack a little shove.

***

They exited the rear door. George led Jack to the car and made him sit in the back. He then drove out the parking lot and headed down Western Ave to Fullerton, then west.

"Hey, aren't we going downtown?" Jack asked.

George didn't answer.

"Did you hear me?

George glared at him in the rear-view mirror.

Minutes ticked by. "Who the hell are you? Jack asked.

"You have a short memory."

Jack rubbed his handcuffed hands against the back of the seat. If George wasn't FBI or a cop, Jack paused... after all these years? The sonofabitch was ... No. He sucked in air and stared at the back of his head.

It seemed like an hour passed. The police scanner came to life. A shooting of a female victim had occurred outside a bar west of the Belmont police station. George made a sharp turn and headed north and then east. It took twenty to thirty minutes to get there. He parked across the sign in the window that flashed Tracy's. He climbed out and took the keys. Minutes later, he slid back into the driver's seat. "Damn fucking fool." He gunned the engine. "The fucking ambulance left to Advocate Illinois Masonic," he mumbled to himself. "Shit."

"Why are we going there?" Jack asked.

"Shut up."

They reached the hospital. George pushed him out of the car.

"You do anything stupid…" He used his forefinger and thumb to imitate a gun.

George took the handcuffs off Jack and walked behind him. He could feel George's breath. George flashed his ID to a woman at Information.

"Who's your friend?" the woman asked.

"He's with me."

"I get that."

"We need the patient to make an identification of the shooter." He raised his eyebrows toward Jack.

"Oh, okay," and directed them to the elevator.

George showed his IDs to a nurse outside of pre-op. She nodded and didn't ask questions. "If you need me," she said, "I'll be down the hall. I'm going for coffee."

George waited until the nurse left. He turned to Jack. "See the woman on the gurney inside that room? I'm going to have a chat. You are going to stay outside by the glass door. If you move, both you and the girl are dead. Is there anything you don't understand?"

Jack gave him an icy stare. Shooter? Him? Another frame-up. Jack shifted his weight. *The world has gone mad. This can't be happening.*

"You know I had nothing to do with this."

George smirked. "We'll see."

George went into the room. Jack focused on the woman. *Holy shit*, he knew her, but couldn't remember from where. He listened to George's one-sided conversation. The bastard called her by her first name. *Yes.* His memory clicked…

Fred's funeral. That was Fred's daughter lying there. Jack saw George draw from his pocket a syringe and a small bottle. *No he's not...*

"Hey!" Jack yelled. "What the fuck are you doing? She's got nothing to do with me." He took a step toward George.

George looked up and let the bottle fall. His hand dropped to his side. Was he grabbing for his gun? Jack didn't wait to find out. He dived and knocked him down. They rolled on the floor and slammed into the gurney. The fight spilled into the hallway and toward an open elevator door. Alarms from the stuck elevator covered the sounds of their grunts. Jack slammed him down again. This time, George hit his head and appeared stunned. As Jack rummaged through his pockets, the sonofabitch found a second wind and kicked Jack in the balls. He doubled over and George charged. He landed a fist to George's face. Blood poured from George's nose as he stumbled. Jack grabbed him and shoved him hard through the opened elevator door. He fell down the shaft. Jack shuddered and then patted himself. It just as easily could have been him.

***

Two hours later, Jack got out of a cab. He was at County Hospital by himself.

He lit a Marlborough and inhaled deeply. Then he flicked the cigarette to the ground and rubbed it out with his shoe. He looked up at the night sky. His past...his goddamn past clung like a second skin...no matter where he went or what country he was in. He had tried hiding, running away, but like his father's Judaism, the shadows followed. Now the bastards wanted vengeance not only on him but anyone connected to him. He wasn't going to let that happen.

He felt a chill as he walked into the emergency room of

the hospital. The entranceway on a Friday night looked like a *M\*A\*S\*H* unit. Gurneys and people were everywhere. Nurses attached portable IV's and yelled orders to move patients. A woman in scrubs raced by him.

"Excuse me," he said, "I know you're busy."

She stopped and scowled at him.

"What floor—"

She put her hand up. "I don't have time for this. Someone should be at Admitting. It's around the corner."

Before he could thank her, she was gone. He pushed his way out and saw the sign. A computer silently flashed on the ledge of the counter but Jack didn't see any human. In fact, no one seemed to be in charge. He turned the computer toward him and entered a name. The cursor blinked twice. Then as if it received inspiration from above, spit out the room number and floor. He didn't move for a moment.

He stared at the screen, then memorized the information and pressed delete. He took a breath and patted his waist. The gun rested beneath his jacket. It was another gift from the late George. Then he hurried to the elevator. She was there on the fourth floor. God, he hoped he was in time.

## Chapter Sixty

# 2015 - Chicago

Billy Dee pressed down on the gas pedal. He'd had been driving this crazy all night long. Thank God there was no traffic. He made it from his house to County Hospital in twenty minutes. He hated the place. The mass of humanity, the senseless injuries, and various diseases made him fearful and sad. He avoided touching anything.

"Shit." He stood outside the front door for a few seconds trying to figure how to open it without gripping the handle. His hand was about to touch when someone walked out. *Thank God.* He braced himself for the turmoil inside.

He eased his way through the crowd and found the admitting desk. He looked around but no one was there. Then he saw a computer. It was on. *What the hell?* He typed in Melissa's name while keeping an eye out for admission's staff. The information popped on the screen.

He took the elevator to the fourth floor. The nurse's station was empty. *What is going on? Where is everyone?* He checked to see if any security guards were on duty. The floor was quiet except for the snores of sleeping patients and beeping machines. He walked down the corridor with his right hand resting on the butt of his gun. He passed room 404. 406 must be around the next hallway. As he turned the corner, he saw the area was dark except for a nightlight. He gripped his weapon.

He hurled himself into the room. He stretched out his arms, pointed the gun at the bed, then the window, then the bathroom. The place was empty. His heart was hammering in his chest. He was too old for this. Did he misread the computer? Where the fuck were Majuski and Melissa? He scratched his head and closed in on the bed. He bent down to see if anything was underneath.

*My God.*

He went for the object. It was a service revolver similar to his. He bolted from the room. An exit sign at the end of the hall was lit. *They took the goddamn stairs.* He surprised himself when he broke into a run. He threw open the stair-well door and heard the clatter of footsteps.

"Stay where you are." He recognized Majuski's voice. "I've got Rakow and the girl. It won't take much for her not to make it, and Rakow ain't too good either. Go back where you came from and everything will be good."

Billy Dee edged up to the handrail and peered through the gaps in the stairwell. The three of them were two flights down.

"You're out of luck, Majuski. Backup is on the way. You got no place to go. Throw your gun down and put your hands where I can see them."

"Why would I do that? Holy shit…you're not dead?" Majuski kept his gun trained on Rakow and Melissa. "I injected you with enough insulin… Well, you're one fucking lucky dude. If you want them to be as fortunate, get the fuck away."

Majuski glanced up for a second. As he did, Rakow lunged toward him. A shot rang out. Someone screamed.

Billy Dee raced down the stairs. He found Majuski sprawled on the steps and not breathing. Melissa gripped the handrail. Rakow knelt by Majuski.

"What the hell happened?" Billy Dee asked.

Jack took rapid breaths. "When—Majuski—looked—up—" Jack stopped and grabbed more air. "I grabbed—the—barrel and as we struggled—the gun—went off."

Doors opened on other floors and four security guards came running to the scene.

One of the guards asked, "What's going on? I heard a shot." His hand moved toward his weapon.

Billy Dee went slowly into his pocket and pulled out his badge. He held it up. "I'm a cop. Call 911, and don't touch a thing," he warned.

Jack grabbed his side and sank to the floor.

Billy Dee spotted blood on Rakow's shirt. "Oh shit."

Jack whispered his words. "I found Melissa's room, Majuski was there." Jack stopped. He balled his fist "He...shot me... going for...my gun." A small smile played on Jack's lips. "Hey, one for two...tonight. Not bad... for an old baseball player." He coughed. "The son of a bitch won't...hurt you or...anyone else. I'm done... running." He wheezed, "My father... saw hell... and survived."

Melissa hobbled over. "You got to pull through, Uncle Jack."

Jack gasped for breath.

"*Nooo*," Melissa cried.

Jack rolled onto his back. His hand was at his side. The blood spread from the wound, turning his shirt dark red. "Sorry about...interview I promised..." He tried to swallow. He couldn't. He motioned Melissa to come close. "I...want to tell...your dad..."

"What?"

He didn't answer.

She looked at Jack then at Billy Dee. "Is he..."

Billy Dee bent over Jack and felt for a pulse. "I'm sorry." He straightened. "My God." He swallowed hard. He didn't want to show emotion. He turned to Melissa. "Lean on me. I'll take you back to your room."

He wrapped his arm around her waist. "You need to rest." He eased her gently up the stairs and got her into bed. He stood over her. He should leave. The detectives would take her statement as well as his. And the captain back at the station would have his ass. But Melissa called him Uncle Jack." Why?

"Do you want to ask me something, Billy Dee?"

He stroked his chin. "I do. I need to make sense of all this. What did Jack mean? And why did you call him uncle?"

A smile crossed her face. "My purse, God willing, is in that drawer. Could you get it?"

"Sure." He stepped over and opened the drawer. "It's still here," and gave it to her.

She dumped the contents on the bed and rummaged through them.

"What are you looking for?"

"A goddamn envelope."

"You've got a lot of junk in that thing. Let me help."

She continued searching. "Here." She handed a faded document to him.

"Hold on." He fished his glasses out of his shirt pocket and put them on. "What is this?" He tried to read it. "This ain't English."

She took the paper back. "It's a Polish birth certificate. My father's. The name on it says Fryderyk Rakowski. Frederick in English."

He let the words sink in. "You mean..."

"Rakow was shortened from Rakowski. Jack's father, Pyotr, changed the name after coming to the US. The war separated Pyotr, my grandfather, from my dad. Pyotr had gone to Germany after Dad was born and somehow survived. After the war, he never found his first wife, Grunia, or his son, Frederick. Jack and Fred were half-brothers but never knew. I did a lot of digging for the interview with Jack that never happened."

"Well, I'll be…"

Melissa leaned back in her bed. "It's a shame. They were good together. Their lives… Who knows? Maybe Dad could have helped."

Billy Dee glanced at the birth certificate lying on the bed. "Now that's a story."

"Yeah it is. My father once said Jack's life was more like a movie. He was right."

Made in the USA
Middletown, DE
09 July 2021